Behind the Seams

A Southern Quilting Mystery, Volume 18

Elizabeth Craig

Published by Elizabeth Craig, 2023.

This is a work of fiction. Similarities to real people, places, or events are entirely coincidental.

BEHIND THE SEAMS

First edition. February 28, 2023.

Written by Elizabeth Craig.

To Cindy. Thanks for the idea!

Chapter One

Beatrice looked at her list and then at her suitcase. Even though she'd carefully used her master packing list, she still had the uneasy feeling she was forgetting something.

She was staring at the unassuming bag with her eyes narrowed and mouth twisted when Wyatt, her husband, stuck his head into their bedroom.

He chuckled, eyes crinkling at the sides. "You look ferocious. What's that suitcase done, now?"

Beatrice smiled back at him. "Oh, nothing, as usual. I just have the feeling I've forgotten something. Even though I'm working from my trusty list."

She waved the list at him, and Wyatt took it gently from her hand. He put on his reading glasses and studied it.

"I think I see the problem," he said with a frown of his own. "The list is the problem, not you. 'Black pumps?' 'Presentation on USB?' These are things I wouldn't necessarily think of when packing for a quilting retreat."

Beatrice took the list back. "It was my master list for work travel. I did a lot of speaking at other art museums on folk art. I crossed those things off, though."

Wyatt nodded. "You definitely did. But if I were the one looking at it, I would get confused."

"Making an updated packing list for traveling is one of those tasks I never seem to get around to. I think I need to have different kinds—maybe one for regular vacation travel and one for something like this . . . a quilt retreat."

Wyatt said, "You're not forgetting your *quilt*, are you?"

Beatrice's eyes grew wide. "For heaven's sake. That's exactly what I'm forgetting. I got so caught up in organizing and packing fabrics and notions that I completely forgot about the quilt itself. I guess I'd have been sitting around, twiddling my thumbs the entire weekend."

She walked into the living room and came back with her quilt-in-progress.

"What's the pattern?" asked Wyatt curiously. "Is it something hard or easy?"

"It's actually something pretty difficult." She carefully put the quilt into a large tote bag. "At first, I thought I'd do something easy this weekend. I thought about all the time we might spend developing friendships and hanging out with Piper. But then I realized the whole focus is quilting, so I might as well tackle something a little more challenging. If I go slow, that's fine. At least I'd have gotten started with it. Plus, if I ran into any trouble, there would be a slew of people there to help me out. And it's not *too* hard. There's no paper piecing involved."

"I'm not sure what paper piecing is, but it sounds like something that's good to avoid," said Wyatt, his eyes crinkling again. "Well, I'll let you double-check your list again. I'm going to switch on the weather."

"Again?" Beatrice raised her eyebrows. "It seems like you've been glued to it lately. Surely, it hasn't changed much since last night."

"You're probably right. I'll give it a check anyway, though. The mountains can be unpredictable."

While Wyatt headed into the living room to pull up the weather on the television, Beatrice gave her belongings one last going over. Noo-noo, her corgi, was watching her intently. She was never a fan of seeing luggage pulled out. She seemed to hope that if she stayed between Beatrice and the door, Beatrice wouldn't forget to bring her along.

Beatrice saw her plaintive eyes and stooped down to give her a rub. "It'll be okay," she said in a soothing voice, as the little dog gave her a mournful look in return. "I'm only going for a few days. You'll be here with Wyatt. Then I'll be back, safe and sound."

Noo-noo didn't look convinced, but lay her sable and white head down on Beatrice's feet and enjoyed the rubbing.

Wyatt came back in, looking rather grim. "The weather has taken a detour, unfortunately. It doesn't look good."

"Really? What are they saying? Storms?"

He shook his head. "Not just storms. Snowstorms. Are you sure the retreat hasn't been cancelled?"

Beatrice pulled her phone out of her purse and opened her text messages and emails. She shook her head. "No. They'd have texted or emailed if they had. And Meadow would have been sure to call, full of indignation. Besides, the weather forecasters have been wrong about the weather for weeks. I'm starting to feel like they must have stock in the area grocery stores because they're making everyone run out to buy bread and milk."

Wyatt still seemed worried. "You don't think the weekend should be rescheduled? Just in case?"

Beatrice shook her head. "I'm sure the retreat wouldn't refund us the money at this point. I have to admit that it would have been nicer to go to a lake retreat in the summer instead of the winter, though. Then we wouldn't be dealing with these sorts of issues at all."

"Why were the Village Quilters interested in going in the winter?"

Beatrice sighed. "Well, they definitely sold us on it with their pictures of big fireplaces, firepits, and the promise of s'mores. But what really clinched the deal was that it was half-price in the off-season."

"I can understand that. And it does sound cozy there. You could read by the fire if you're not quilting."

Beatrice chuckled. "I almost ended up doing a *lot* of reading, considering I nearly forgot to bring my quilt. Let's hope there's nothing else I've forgotten." She reached over and put her arms around her husband. "Don't worry about the weather. We'll be fine."

"You've got your cell phone charger?"

She nodded. "I do. I've checked that three times. I'll give you updates from the quilting front."

Wyatt looked down at their corgi. "Someone else looks worried about you going."

Beatrice bent down to pick up Noo-noo, cradling her on the bed. The little dog looked up at her with solemn eyes.

"I'll be back soon," said Beatrice. "I'd smuggle you into the retreat if I didn't think I'd get caught."

Noo-noo gave her an understanding doggy smile.

Beatrice looked at her watch. "I suppose I'd better head on out, since I'm picking everyone up."

"Not *everyone*, surely."

"No. Not everybody could make it. Edgenora, for one, is staying at home and June Bug is staying put to manage the bakery. But in terms of my car, it will feel like everyone is in it," said Beatrice with a laugh. "It's going to be a full car. I've got Meadow, Piper, and Miss Sissy."

Wyatt frowned. "How on earth are you going to fit everyone's luggage in there?"

"Oh, Posy is borrowing a friend's van and we're all putting our bags in there. There was no way to make it work otherwise."

After eating a very quick snack and giving Wyatt and Noo-noo hugs, Beatrice headed off to Meadow's house, which was the meeting place for the group. She put her suitcase into Posy's van.

Beatrice's daughter, Piper, gave her a hug. "How are you, Mama?"

"More important, how are *you*? This is your longest time away from Will, isn't it?"

Piper smiled ruefully. "Don't remind me. I already boo-hooed after leaving home. It's going to be a great break, I know. But I'm going to miss him and Ash, too."

Meadow, who was Will's other grandmother, overheard Piper. Her eyes immediately filled with tears. "I know! I was thinking just a little while ago how much I was going to miss the baby. It'll be hard."

Beatrice said, "It's only for a few nights. I think it will be good for us."

Meadow looked exceedingly doubtful about this. Also, she appeared to be reaching for her cell phone, likely to show off the most recent editions of her photo albums of Will.

Beatrice quickly interjected, "We should probably get going, shouldn't we? Wyatt was talking about the possibility of bad weather."

Meadow put a finger over her lips. "Don't say that too loud! I've been on a mission to make sure Ramsay doesn't hear a whisper about possible snow. With his job, he's seen a lot of awful accidents due to bad weather. He'd be worried sick about us."

Ramsay was the local police chief and Beatrice had no doubt that he'd probably seen his share of car accidents, weather-related and otherwise.

Piper looked concerned. "You don't think there's going to be a problem on the roads, do you?"

Beatrice shook her head. "The forecasters have been wrong so many times lately. I'm sure we'll be fine. You packed plenty of warm clothes, though, didn't you?"

Piper nodded. "I figured it might be pretty windy, next to the lake."

Meadow said, "We'll just have to cuddle up in front of the firepit! I'm looking forward to having some s'mores."

The mention of food brought Miss Sissy, the guild's oldest member, hurrying over. She must have been expecting a pre-trip snack because she not only looked disappointed at the lack of s'mores, but looked furious at having been deceived.

"We'll have them at the retreat," said Meadow. "That's what the brochures promised, anyway."

Miss Sissy's expression implied that the organizers would have a lot to answer for if the s'mores didn't materialize soon after arrival.

Posy climbed back into the van and gave a cheerful toot of her horn. “Ready for a quilting adventure?” she called out through her open window.

“Ready!” said Meadow. “Let’s get this show on the road.”

So they set out with Posy’s van leading and Beatrice right behind.

Chapter Two

It was a beautiful, crisp mountain day and hard to believe there was any bad weather in the forecast. The sun was beaming from a bright blue sky.

They were hardly more than a few minutes into the trip when Meadow produced a large wicker basket. "Is everyone ready for a road trip snack?"

Beatrice glanced at her in disbelief. "We've barely left your driveway!"

"Which makes it the perfect time to eat. That way, we'll be hungry by the time we arrive in case they've made something delicious as an arrival snack."

Piper said, "I thought the trip to the lake was only about an hour and a half or so."

"Y'all are no fun at all!" said Meadow in mock anger. "And I've been baking like crazy for this road trip."

Miss Sissy reached out her arthritic hands for the basket, fully intending on consuming its contents by herself.

Beatrice quickly interjected, "I didn't say I didn't want any." Meadow was an amazing cook.

"Me either," Piper quickly added. "Save some for me."

Meadow looked appeased. "Good. There are three different kinds of cookies in there, brownies, and some party mix."

As usual, the food was all delicious. But Meadow didn't want to stop there. "I thought we might sing. That's always fun during a road trip."

Beatrice was dubious about that. "I can speak for Piper and me and say neither of us can sing."

"Oh, I find that hard to believe."

Beatrice glanced in the rearview mirror at Piper in the backseat. "Let's give her a sample of 'She'll be Comin' Round the Mountain.'"

After fifteen seconds of a rousing rendition of the folk song, Meadow had winced and Miss Sissy hissed from the backseat.

Beatrice and Piper chuckled. "I told you it was bad," said Beatrice.

"There are different levels of bad," said Meadow. "That was in the awful range." Then she brightened. "Something else Ramsay and I liked to do with Ash when we traveled was road games."

Piper said, "Too funny! We played those, too. Which ones did Ash like best?"

"All of them! But the one that kept him the most occupied was the license plate game. He would try to get as many states as he could on long trips. On our shorter trips, he'd shoot for the whole alphabet from the first letters of different license plates he saw. But here, considering there's not much traffic, we could try to get the alphabet from any signs we see."

Beatrice was exempted from the game since she was driving, and everyone wanted her to keep her eyes on the curvy mountain road. But the rest of them played the license plate game—a game that got progressively harder as they moved from well-traveled roads to more rural ones. Miss Sissy and her sharp eyes ended up winning her the game, and a round of applause.

"Does this conference center only do quilting retreats?" asked Meadow. "It seems like it's in the middle of nowhere."

Piper said, "From what I saw online, they have conferences there all year round. It looked very popular; their online calendar was booked up, even in the winter."

Meadow said, "That's another reason we needed to go. We couldn't have rescheduled to a different weekend if the place was always booked. Plus, I'm sure we wouldn't have been able to get our deposit back. Besides, the sky is blue as blue can be."

Beatrice frowned. "Is it? It looks like it's getting cloudier to the east."

"White, puffy clouds. Nothing too ominous," deemed Meadow with a sniff.

But, by the time they'd reached the retreat, heavier clouds had rolled in. Meadow, naturally, was determined to put an optimistic spin on things. "It'll keep us from getting sunburned."

Beatrice felt it was unlikely that the group would get sunburned in January, but she wisely kept her thoughts to herself.

She parked the car, following the directions of one of the staff. Posy parked on the other side of her, and everyone headed to the van to grab their things.

A staff member got them checked in and assigned them cabins.

Meadow said, "This is a huge place! Who else is here?"

The staff member said, "We have your guild and one other quilting guild for the weekend. The entire retreat grounds won't be open, but you'll have a well-stocked conference room."

Meadow frowned. "Just one other guild here? I was thinking there might be more."

"There were supposed to be three others, but they decided to cancel because of the weather forecast," the young woman said.

Miss Sissy growled at the mention of the forecast, startling the staff member a bit.

Piper said quickly, "Does it look like there will be snow?"

The young woman gave her a reassuring smile. "I'm sure it'll be fine. We're right on the lake, after all. The lake ordinarily keeps us from getting any wintry weather here."

The quilters took their bags to their assigned cabins and spent a few minutes unpacking. Beatrice worried the cabins might be a little rustic, but was pleased to see that the one she and Piper shared was very well-appointed. There was a warm rug on the floor, slippers and robes for guests, two separate bedrooms, and even a small sitting area between them with a kitchenette.

Piper said, "This is a lot nicer than I thought it would be. I was worried it would be more like camping."

"I was a little concerned about that, too. But I guess the conference center hosts all sorts of different groups, so they'd want to make sure everyone is comfortable. Want to go explore?"

Piper said, "I'd definitely like to take a look at where we'll be quilting. It sounds like we don't have the whole run of the place, though."

Beatrice flipped through the welcome packet the staff had given her when she arrived. "There's a map here. They've crossed off the buildings and areas that are closed off."

With that, they headed over to the conference room set up for quilting. Inside, there were long tables, sewing machines, ironing boards with irons, a collection of notions, and even quilts on the walls.

Piper studied the quilts. "Were these from former retreats?"

"Maybe the conference center purchased them. They definitely help set the mood."

There was a wall of windows from floor to ceiling on one side that looked out on the lake and the surrounding mountains. Beatrice was sure it was probably a great view in the summer when it would overlook children swimming, sailboats, and picnics. But in the dead of winter, it lent a rather bleak feel to the space.

Piper shivered, seeming to feel it, too. "I'm getting chilly just looking out. Or is it cold in this room?"

"I think they might have to turn up the heat. There's definitely a draft in here when the wind blows."

And the wind was blowing constantly.

Piper glanced up at the skylights cut out of the ceiling. "Look how fast the clouds are moving."

Sure enough, the wind was pushing huge puffy clouds across the sky.

Beatrice made a face. "I wonder if that's the snowstorm moving in."

"Snow, I can handle. If it's ice, though . . . all bets are off."

For the first time, Beatrice felt a frisson of unease. Ice was a frequent problem in the mountains and was much more treacherous than snow. Driving in snow wasn't a problem. Driving in ice was something else completely. Plus, ice often meant that the electricity could go off.

Her uneasiness must have been reflected on her face because Piper swiftly said, "Let's not worry about something that probably won't even happen. Maybe the wind will blow the storm out of here and further down the road. I know—let's set out our quilting stuff before anyone else does. Then we can sit together."

Beatrice smiled at her. "Sounds like a great idea."

And it did. One of the main reasons she wanted to come on this retreat was so she and Piper could spend more time together. The quilting was decidedly secondary. Although she got to see Piper several times a week, this would be her first one-on-one time with her in a long while. She loved her grandson, but really appreciated the opportunity for her and Piper to visit with each other while Will stayed with Ash.

As they walked back to their cabin to get their quilting bags, Piper asked, "Who's rooming with whom?"

Beatrice considered this. "Well, we know Savannah and Georgia will be together." They were sisters, and it made the most sense. "I'm guessing Meadow and Posy are sharing another cabin, unless one of them is sharing a cabin with Miss Sissy."

Piper snorted. "I doubt anyone wants to share with Miss Sissy. We've all heard her snoring in the Patchwork Cottage over the years. You'd have to wear earplugs to get any sleep, even from another room, and I'm not even sure that would work."

They gathered their supplies and started setting everything up in the conference room, chatting as they did.

"Smart girls!" said a voice behind them.

They turned to see Meadow standing there. "Look at you two," she said. "Getting all organized and set up early. My stuff is a total mess. I didn't pack until late, so I ended up just randomly stuffing things into my suitcase and my tote bag."

Piper said, "You've got time to unpack now."

Meadow gave her a rueful look. "That's what Posy is doing. It would be the smart thing for me to do because I feel really disorganized. But after spending so much time in the car, I had the itch to walk around and explore."

"Did you grab your map?" asked Beatrice, indicating the slip of paper from the welcome pack.

Meadow said, "We have a map?"

"In the welcome pack."

Meadow shook her head. "I hadn't gotten that far. I thought I'd just head outside and wander around. It's a good size place, but it seems like it's pretty self-contained, so I shouldn't get lost. And I can stretch my legs. I feel sort of weird walking without Boris and Cammie, though. They're my walking buddies."

Boris was Meadow's huge dog and Cammie was her rescued little one who now seemed to rule the roost.

Piper asked, "You walk both of them at the same time? How does that work? I know Boris likes to yank you down the road. And Cammie has such short legs, I'd think she wouldn't be able to keep up."

"If I were on roller skates, Boris would pull me all over town! Honestly, it would probably be a better way for me to get places. But you wouldn't believe how good he is when I'm walking Cammie. She keeps him in his place. He always behaves himself when they're together. Unless there's a squirrel. If he sees a squirrel, then all bets are off. Then Cammie snarls at him for dashing ahead and pulling me and her along."

"Is he chastened when she snarls at him?" asked Beatrice.

"Boy, is he! He starts walking with his head down and his tail between his legs." Meadow chuckled at the thought. "I'm going to miss that big lug here."

Beatrice and Piper smiled. "You make it sound like we're gone for a month. We're only here for the weekend."

Meadow brightened. "That's true. And I'm looking forward to meeting the other quilt guild members. Have you seen anybody yet?"

Beatrice shook her head. "Piper and I were too busy getting unpacked. And no one else has come over to the conference room yet."

Meadow said, "At first, I was disappointed that the weather scared off the other guilds. I'd figured we were going to have maybe fifty quilters or more here, but it looks like it's probably going to be fewer than twenty. Then I decided we should make the best of the situation and get close with the one other guild that's here. I was thinking if we all hit it off, they could be our sister guild! We could even have them as pen pals or have joint quilt shows with them."

Beatrice thought this type of friendship was a lot to ask for during a brief weekend when they were planning to spend a lot of time working on their projects.

Meadow, however, was still unpacking this idea. "Maybe I shouldn't sit next to the two of you. Maybe I should make a point to sit in the middle of women from the other guild."

Piper said, "That's a great idea, Meadow! You can be the ambassador from our group."

Meadow seemed to like the sound of that. She puffed up at the idea of this role. "That's what I'll do, then. I'll wait until a few of them have arrived in the conference room and then I'll plop my stuff down right in the center." She walked back toward the door. "In the meantime, I'm going to explore."

"Do you want to take my map?" Beatrice waved it at her.

Meadow shook her head and said with a grin, "Nope. I'll just let serendipity work its magic. Toodle-oo!"

Piper chuckled. "Why do I have the feeling she's going to get lost?"

"It's a foregone conclusion," said Beatrice. "Her sense of direction isn't great to start with, especially in an unfamiliar place."

Piper said, "Was there anything else in that welcome packet that we should pay attention to?"

"There was some sort of agenda in there, I think."

Piper said, "I'll pull it out."

She flipped through a few papers in the manila envelope until she found the schedule. "It looks like we've got an orientation in a few minutes."

Beatrice raised an eyebrow. "An orientation? For a quilt retreat?"

Piper studied the paper. "I think it's more about the amenities here. What time meals are served, the structure of the day, and things like that."

"Got it. I guess we can fill Meadow in on the details."

Piper grinned. "Maybe one of the staff members will herd her over there."

But there was no sign of Meadow when they got settled over in a small auditorium where the orientation was being held. The rest of the Village Quilters were there, though, and Beatrice and Piper sat next to them.

"Have you seen Meadow?" asked Posy, her sweet features creased with concern.

Beatrice nodded. "She said she was going to explore the retreat grounds."

"With a map?" asked Posy in a hopeful tone.

Piper said, "She decided not to take one. Maybe she'll realize no one is walking around outside and will join us soon."

Georgia, who was sitting next to Posy, leaned over. "Looks like the other guild here is called 'The Sew and Sews.' Isn't that cute?"

Beatrice nodded. "Very clever. It looks like there's six of them here, unless some of their group is missing."

Georgia said, "Part of me is a little disappointed that there aren't more quilters here. I guess the weather forecast really scared people off."

"Luckily, it's an absolutely beautiful day," said Posy, lifting up her chin and looking contentedly through the skylight above. "The sky is a gorgeous blue." Then she made the tiniest of frowns. "Wow, the clouds sure are moving quickly. I guess the wind is clearing out the sky."

Beatrice had thought that perhaps the wind was blowing the clouds *in*, but she didn't want to say anything.

A woman standing at the front of the room cleared her throat and said, "May I have your attention, please? We'll go ahead and start."

Chapter Three

The woman was in her thirties with thick dark hair and a rather stern expression. She waited a moment until the conversations quieted down. "Thank you. My name is Starr Brook and I'm the director of the Lakeside Conference Center. I hope you'll all enjoy your time here."

She went on to outline the menu, cafeteria hours, the location of the first aid area, activities that were offered when members weren't quilting, and other aspects of the retreat.

"Are there any questions?" Starr asked smoothly.

One of the women from the Sew and Sews raised her hand and Starr nodded at her.

"Have you seen an updated weather forecast?" the woman asked. "It looked like we might be in for bad weather."

Starr nodded, saying briskly, "Of course, our team here has been staying on top of the forecast. We would have cancelled the weekend altogether if there had been any threat of inclement weather. We feel confident that the storm is going to pass north of us."

The quilter looked relieved.

A voice from behind them boomed, "Well, here you all are! I've been looking everywhere for signs of life and couldn't find a single soul."

Beatrice winced. It was Meadow, of course.

Starr narrowed her eyes, giving Meadow a chilly smile. "I'm afraid you've missed the orientation—we were just wrapping up."

Meadow didn't look fazed at all. "Oh, no worries. One of my friends will fill me in." She waved at the row of Village Quilters.

A minute later, Starr had walked over to speak with the Sew and Sews and the quilters were helping to catch Meadow up with what she'd missed.

"Sounds easy-peasy," she said with a shrug. "If it's all on the piece of paper anyway, why did we need to hear it?"

It was, Beatrice admitted, a good question. But perhaps there were legalities involved on the conference center's side.

Piper looked carefully at the agenda. "Looks like the dining hall is going to be opening up in a few minutes."

Meadow brightened. "Good! I'm starved."

Beatrice looked at the schedule. "It looks like it'll be open for a while. I'm not quite ready to eat yet since we had those snacks in the car."

"You should take a walk around the grounds," said Meadow. "This is a pretty place. The sun came out briefly and shone on the lake and over the tops of the mountains. There were all kinds of birds flying by. It was really gorgeous out there." She stopped and then said excitedly, "Look! Some of the Sew and Sews are coming over to meet us!"

Meadow sounded like a girl in the lunchroom, seeing the cool girls coming over to talk. Just the same, though, Beatrice smoothed her platinum-white hair in case it had gotten blown by the swift breeze on the way over.

There was indeed a group of them walking their way. The person in the front looked to be in her thirties with very blonde hair and dramatic makeup. She grinned at them, but the grin looked mischievous instead of welcoming. She drawled, "I understand you're the Village Quilters. What village is it that you hail from?"

Meadow was practically falling all over herself to answer. "From Dappled Hills. You might not have heard of it."

But the younger woman cut her off. "I know all about Dappled Hills. Vacation-type area in the mountains. Nice. I'm Aspen." She gestured to the rest of the group to introduce themselves, and they quickly did. It appeared she was the leader of the guild, despite the fact that she was clearly younger than they were. Beatrice wondered if that rankled some of the other women.

One of them definitely seemed annoyed upon a closer look. She was a very thin woman with black hair and a dour expression who introduced herself as Olive.

Meadow asked breathlessly, "Where are you all from? Are you from the mountains, too? I was thinking we could even be sister guilds or set up sort of a pen pal thing. Maybe we could even have quilt shows together!"

The group looked somewhat overwhelmed by Meadow's effusive ideas. One of the quilters said hesitantly, "We're from the midsection of the state. In a small town near Greensboro." She paused and then added, "It might be fun to do things together, of course."

Beatrice said, "We could play that by ear. I'm guessing right now we're all ready to get some quilting done."

Aspen, the younger quilter, smirked. "Maybe later. Right now, I'm interested in the relaxation part of the retreat. I brought plenty of vodka and mixers. Anybody up for a drink?"

The Village Quilters all looked rather startled, Beatrice thought. Everyone did enjoy alcohol, but they were more the glass-of-wine-with-dinner types. Now it was lunchtime, and she was pretty sure the thought of having a drink hadn't crossed any of their minds.

Olive, the one who'd appeared irritated by Aspen earlier said, "I think we'd rather wait until later. We just got here, after all. I was thinking about going over to the dining hall and having some lunch."

The rest of the Sew and Sews murmured agreement.

Aspen's mouth twisted. "I see. Okay, I guess I'm on my own, then. See you later."

Beatrice felt there was a palpable sense of relief from the Sew and Sews when Aspen left them.

Meadow had regained her enthusiasm after looking flummoxed by Aspen for a bit. "So, lunch? I was just telling the others how hungry I am. We had appetizers in the car on the way over, but all they did was whet my appetite. I'm ready for some real food! Have y'all ever been here before for a retreat? Was the food any good?"

Meadow's standards for good food were probably pretty high, considering what an excellent cook she was. Beatrice was interested to hear the answer. Food could definitely make or break a retreat.

Apparently, only one of the Sew and Sews had been to the retreat before. She said, "It's pretty good. Not award-winning food, of course, but perfectly serviceable."

Meadow looked crestfallen. Her impression of *serviceable* was not very good.

Regardless, most of the women headed toward the dining hall. Meadow said, "Come on, Beatrice. At least have a snack over there."

Considering the rest of the Village Quilters were already heading in that direction, Beatrice decided to come along. But soon, she was sure she'd feel the pull of the cabin. Being with a large group had that effect on her. Every once in a while, she was going to want to retreat to a little peace and quiet.

The dining hall was a large and impressive room with rustic chandeliers hanging between large skylights. More floor to ceiling windows showcased the lake view. Now, however, the brief spell of pretty weather seemed to be at an end as large gray clouds were taking over the sky.

The others were more interested in what was on the buffet table. And Beatrice had to admit it looked good . . . more than serviceable, in her estimation. There were fresh fruits, different types of nuts, salad fixings, pasta salads, and cold cuts for sandwiches.

Only Savannah and Meadow looked disappointed. Meadow liked heavy, fried foods, and Savannah had a tendency toward junk food of all descriptions. But the others were loading their plates with a variety of offerings. Miss Sissy was already seated and devouring everything in front of her.

As the Village Quilters settled into seats at the large round tables that populated the big room, the Sew and Sews started sitting next to them. Piper said quietly to Beatrice, "They seem pretty outgoing, don't they? That makes things easier."

Beatrice wondered if it really did. Again, she felt as if she might want to put her feet up for a while after lunch. Particularly considering how much food she was consuming. Any thought of a small snack had flown out the window when she'd seen the buffet.

Piper could apparently read her thoughts, because she said, "I'm sure we won't be socializing all day. On the agenda, it looked like we have some free time after lunch."

Beatrice gave her a rueful grin. "Am I that obvious? I guess I must have gotten out of the habit of meeting lots of new people at once. And there really aren't that many of them, are there? Maybe six? Still, they almost seem like a hoard."

"A hoard of quilters?" Piper quirked an eyebrow at her.

"Silly, I know. Part of me feels like I'm back in summer camp. Like I'll be writing postcards to my parents after lunch."

Beatrice stopped talking abruptly when two of the Sew and Sews sat next to Piper and her. She smiled at the two women. One was Aspen and the other was a sturdy woman with graying hair, and large glasses.

Aspen carelessly waved a hand in the woman's direction. "This is Cora. Are these seats saved?"

Without waiting for an answer, Aspen sat down next to Beatrice. She glanced at her plate. "Not hungry?"

Beatrice had thought her plate was groaning with food, but Aspen apparently thought otherwise. She had piled her plate high.

"We had snacks in the car on the way over," said Beatrice with a small smile.

Aspen said, "Maybe I'm just hungry because I made time to work out this morning before I left for the retreat." She made a face. "Apparently, the fitness center is one of the areas they closed off, but I worked out in my room with just my body weight."

The other woman, Cora, said, "You've already worked out? You must have gotten up really early for that."

Aspen shrugged. "It's the way to get it done. If you don't exercise when you first get up, you can't count on it happening later on. Your day could get totally sabotaged by something else that comes up."

Piper, whose days frequently were hijacked by her very cute toddler, looked a little envious. "I've been wanting to do some exercising at the start of my day, but it just hasn't worked out."

Aspen gave a quick glance over Piper. "You must have kids."

Piper nodded, smiling, thinking that maybe Aspen was going to talk about hers, too.

"That's where you went wrong," said Aspen with a shrug. "It's a lot easier to get the things you want from life when you don't have children."

Meadow, just putting her plate down on the table, caught the last bit and gave Aspen a horrified look. "What? I simply can't imagine Piper with no children. I wouldn't have my little grandbaby then and neither would Beatrice. He's precious and brilliant, too."

With that and with absolutely no encouragement from Aspen, Meadow plopped down, pulled up a slew of photos on her phone, and subjected Aspen to them for the next five minutes.

Beatrice hid a smile. Aspen deserved it. There was something about the young woman that got under her skin. Her brashness, maybe. At any rate, she was going to try her best to avoid her, if possible.

Aspen finally was able to break away from the impromptu slideshow of baby pictures. She said, "Sure, he's adorable. But I wouldn't trade in my lifestyle for him."

Meadow started spluttering as Aspen continued. "I've got the perfect setup. A big house with its own gym, a media and video game room, and tons of room for me to host. My car isn't any Cheerio-covered minivan, but a totally tricked out Jeep that cost a fortune and is just the way I like it. Nothing tying me down. It's a great life."

There was the sound of breaking glass and a gasp from Cora, whose angry face turned red. "I'm so sorry," she muttered, as she stooped to pick up the broken water glass from the floor.

Before she could touch it, though, the staff swooped in with a broom and pan and efficiently removed the debris.

Aspen rolled her eyes. "Cora has a hard time concealing her envy. Plus, she's clumsy on top of it."

Cora's face flushed even redder and there was fury in her eyes.

As if that wasn't enough drama, a voice hissed angrily behind Beatrice's head. It was Olive, the woman with the dark hair and dour expression and she seemed absolutely furious with Aspen.

"It was my *brother's* money. You're profiteering from that, and you know it. You don't deserve a cent of his money and you did nothing whatsoever to earn it." Streaks of angry red splotched up from her chest and over her face.

Aspen gave her a lazy smile, seemingly unaffected by Olive's tirade. "Are we sure about that?"

Olive's answer to this was to press her lips tightly together and stomp away to another table.

Aspen polished off her food. "Well, I've stirred things up enough around here, I guess. Mission accomplished. See you all later."

Looking satisfied with herself, she strolled away.

Chapter Four

Cora was still flushed from having broken a glass and was now looking even more so with embarrassment. "Sorry about her," she mumbled.

"Goodness! No need to apologize for Aspen. You're not her keeper, after all," said Meadow.

"Is she always like that?" asked Piper sympathetically.

Cora gave Piper and Meadow a grateful smile. "Thanks for understanding. Yes, I'm afraid she's like that most of the time."

Beatrice said, "Maybe she'll settle down when we all start quilting."

Cora gave a tired laugh. "Well, that's optimistic."

Meadow frowned. She never liked to think quilters could be anything but well-behaved. To her, quilting was a noble craft. "Is Aspen new to quilting? Or did she join your guild with some sort of underhanded motivation?"

"Oh, she's not new to quilting. In fact, she's fabulous at it. It almost makes her behavior worthwhile to see her gorgeous quilts. Aspen is a natural. I'll show you some pictures."

Cora fumbled with her phone for a few seconds and then proceeded to bring up some photos. There was a spectacular Christmas quilt covered with embroidered wreaths, stockings, and cozy kitchens. There was also a very modern-looking quilt with a combination of hand-painted background fabric and quilted animals.

"Amazing," breathed Beatrice, making the images on the phone larger.

Piper smiled at Cora. "My mom is a retired art museum curator. I think she's back in that mode."

Beatrice handed the phone to Meadow, who took it eagerly. Beatrice said, "She's certainly very talented. I can see why you said you could put up with her shenanigans to enjoy her quilts."

Cora nodded. "She inspires all of us. When she's not putting down own efforts, of course. Or making mischief. I'm starting to believe the whole reason she came on the retreat was to make trouble. She was even needling us on the way over in the car."

Cora flushed a little. "Anyway, I shouldn't be talking. None of us is perfect, after all. I'd better head back to the cabin and organize my things."

With that, she scurried away.

Piper said in a thoughtful voice, "It sounds like there might be plenty of drama this weekend."

Beatrice sighed, "I hope not. I wanted us to have a relaxing weekend."

Meadow, naturally, wasn't ready to throw in the towel on the retreat. "What do you mean? It's going to be great. Think of all we can learn from Aspen."

"If she's interested in teaching us," said Beatrice wryly.

"Even if she's not, it's still the perfect opportunity to learn something new. I've never gotten the knack of mixing media on a quilt. Maybe Aspen can show us how to integrate hand-painting and quilting. Like you said, Beatrice, she might settle down as soon as the quilting starts."

Beatrice wished she felt that optimistic.

However, things did seem to be a little better when they all headed over to the conference room later on to start their quilting. There was a happy energy in the group . . . everyone was chatting, talking about their current projects, and getting started. The big room was full of color and texture and the happy sounds of quilters at work.

At one point Starr, the retreat manager, came into the room. She stood at the front and said, "Glad to see everyone happy and quilting! Welcome again to Lakeside. There's one thing we like to do here that's an icebreaker activity."

There was a sarcastic moan from Aspen. She said, "Really? Is that necessary?"

Beatrice saw a flush rise up Starr's neck, but she levelly said, "If you'll play along, it might enrich your time here at the retreat."

Aspen muttered something under her breath.

Meadow, always game for any sort of team-building, said brightly, "Let's do it!"

"If everyone could say their name, what they're working on now, and talk a little about their favorite quilt from the past, then," said Starr. "Let's start over here."

So each of the quilters introduced themselves. Beatrice, who had to try harder with names than she used to, jotted down each name and a short description of the quilter in a small notebook she carried with her. She'd met Aspen, Olive, and Cora, of course, but was glad for a refresher on their names. Aside from them, the other Sew and Sews were Ivy, Maggie, and Nicole.

The quilts they were all working on varied. One was a challenging hexagon pattern involving piecing. But another was a frameless machine quilt in bright reds, greens, and purples. Posy was working on an appliqué quilt. And Aspen was working on a minimalist design of moon phases.

Afterward, they all returned to their quilting. But the icebreaker seemed to have worked well. The chatter in the room was louder and conversations between the Village Quilters and the Sew and Sews seemed to have increased in number.

Beatrice, however, couldn't help but steal looks at the big window in front of them. The weather seemed to be taking a turn for the worse. She wondered if it would really pass north of the retreat like Starr had said, or whether they were about to get a lot of winter weather. She told herself not to worry. After all, she had no control over the weather. She might as well just settle in and see what happens.

For the next couple of hours, the room was full of the happy sounds of creative productivity. Beatrice loved having Piper sitting next to her for so long, talking about her toddler son, her hopes for the future, and even just random comments about the quilt she was working on. "I wanted one I could do in my sleep," said Piper wryly. "That way I'm not focusing a hundred percent on it."

Beatrice chuckled. "I went with a completely different mindset and decided to try something challenging. I think I'm ruing that now."

"It's pretty," said Piper, glancing over the blocks. "I love the cheerful colors."

The quilt had earthy colors in shades of green but also sunset colors in reds and oranges.

"I do, too. But there are lots of blocks and lots of seams. And I'm enjoying talking with you too much! I'm going to end up making a mistake."

Piper shrugged. "So what? The quilt will be just as soft and just as cozy when you finish it, even if some of the seams are off."

"Good point," said Beatrice. "And it's not like I'll enter this in a show or anything. It's just going to be thrown on the bed."

After a couple of hours of work, most of the women were ready to take a break. Posy looked out the big windows with concern. "If we're going for a walk, maybe we should do it before the bad weather comes in."

So Beatrice and Posy headed off to explore. Piper begged off, saying she wanted to call in and check on Ash and see how things were going with the baby.

Posy zipped up her puffy coat and then strung a cheerful scarf around her neck. She finished by putting on some heavy gloves.

"You're certainly prepared for whatever weather is thrown our way," said Beatrice.

Posy smiled at her. "It's less preparation and more of just being super-cold all the time. Honestly, there are some days that I could dress like this in my shop, even though I run the heat at the Patchwork Cottage on high. I don't like being cold."

"As I've gotten older, I feel the same way. I used to hate being hot and loved the cold weather. But now, I feel the other way around."

The lake was huge and the gray clouds reflected on the water, lending it an almost eerie effect. Beatrice shivered.

"Want to run get a hat or something?" asked Posy with concern.

"No, I'm all right. I just had a goose walk over my grave, that's all. It feels very isolated out here, doesn't it? I thought there would be a lot more development on this side of the lake. But it seems like this is the only place out here."

Posy nodded. "I spent a little time on the website before we left. It seems the property used to belong to a family. They had quite a few acres here and then sold it all to the people who own the conference center. I guess in the summer, they can host large numbers of guests here."

"I suppose it does make it feel more of a real retreat this way. After all, a retreat implies *withdrawing*, doesn't it? That's certainly what we've done. I feel like we've left most of civilization behind."

Posy laughed. "I don't know if it's that bad. It's pretty civilized at the retreat. Fancy food and nice lodgings." She paused. "I really needed a getaway."

"Everything okay?" asked Beatrice with concern. She had always been very fond of Posy, who remained one of her favorite Village Quilters. Her quiet, sweet manner was endearing, and she was always so supportive and encouraging.

Posy said quickly, "Oh, it's really nothing. I think I've just been burned out lately. You know how much I love the shop, of course. It's been busy recently, though. A good thing for business! But a little tiring for me. You know my helper resigned. She wanted to move to another state to take care of her mom. She's helping out this weekend for me while I'm gone, but then she's finished at the shop."

Beatrice realized that sometimes she wasn't quite as observant as she should be. She had definitely noticed that Posy was on her own in the lively shop much of the time. But she hadn't put two-and-two together to see it would be tough on her to do all the different parts of the business. "Are you looking for someone else to take her place?"

Posy nodded. "But it's not very easy. I'd rather have someone who quilts, too, and it seems like a really tall order." She quickly waved her hand to dismiss the problem. "Let's not worry about it now. I'm sure it will all work out."

Beatrice paused. "You know, maybe I could help you out in the shop in the short term."

"You? But Beatrice, you're so busy. You help out at the church, watch Will, and have family time."

"But I hang out in the Patchwork Cottage all the time, anyway, just to visit with everybody. It wouldn't be forever—just until you can find someone permanent."

Posy beamed at her. "Would you? That would be amazing. I already feel the stress lifting from me. Once we get back, I'll start advertising for some help in earnest."

"And I'll look forward to putting in some hours at my favorite shop," said Beatrice with a smile.

Posy now seemed to have a bounce in her step as they took a walk around the grounds. They saw different cabins, a residence hall, and an office for guest use.

Then Posy paused. "I think I felt a drop."

Beatrice held out her hand. "You're right." She glanced at the pavement. "It looks like freezing rain, not snow."

"Oh no," said Posy. "I hope that won't bring down the power lines."

"I didn't notice a generator on our walk, did you?"

Posy shook her head. "It would be a huge investment. And it's doubtful they usually have a problem with winter storms."

Whatever was falling from the sky, it was cold and wet and the two women hurried back to their cabins.

After a rest in the cabin followed by a good dinner in the dining hall, Beatrice had decided that she'd socialized enough for the day. She was ready to retire to the cabin with her book. Piper said, "I'll try to be quiet when I come back in, in case you're asleep."

"Oh, I have the feeling I'll sleep like a log. Don't worry about me."

But later, at 1:00 a.m., Beatrice was sorry that she'd said anything about sleeping like a log. She must have jinxed herself. She should have remembered that she never slept well the first night in a new place.

Beatrice tried to read for a little while, but found she wasn't getting any sleepier, which is what she wanted. She'd read that it was a good idea to get out of bed if you couldn't sleep. But she wondered if she'd wake up Piper if she wandered into the tiny sitting area between their rooms. Part of her wanted a glass of water, too. There was a kitchenette on one wall of the sitting area but there again she'd be banging around right next to Piper's room. She felt like Piper had to be awake so often in the middle of the night with Will that she deserved a quiet night with no interruptions for once.

Then Beatrice remembered they'd said during the orientation that the conference room would be open twenty-four hours a day for the quilters. She also recalled there was a water cooler in the room. She wasn't completely sure she wanted to quilt until she got sleepy, so she grabbed her book too as she put on her coat and her shoes and left the cabin as quietly as she could.

The first thing she realized when she opened the cabin door was the sense of cold, multiplied by the wind. She took in a deep breath as the frigid air seemed to sweep right through her. The second thing she noticed was that the ground was covered in snow. And what was falling on top of it was sleet. She groaned. This was what she'd been afraid of. No one could navigate in ice and a generous coating of ice could also bring down power lines.

She went back into the cabin to put her boots on, glad that she'd stuck them in the car as a precaution. Then she quietly headed outside again.

A few minutes later, she was opening the door to the conference center. It was dark in the room and very quiet. She was relieved no one else seemed to be having trouble sleeping. She hadn't felt like visiting.

Beatrice fumbled on the wall, feeling for a light switch. Finally, she found it and switched it on. She glanced around for the water cooler and, spotting it, headed over to grab a paper cup and fill it with water.

She turned to find her seat and stopped cold.

There was a body lying on the floor with a pair of shears sticking out of its back.

Chapter Five

Beatrice stood still, shaking. From the blonde hair she saw, she thought it must be Aspen, the abrasive quilter from the day before.

As she stood there, trying to think what to do next, the door opened behind her. Beatrice spun around to see a thin woman with dark hair. She remembered her name was Olive.

The woman frowned at her. "Beatrice, isn't it? What's going on?"

Beatrice pointed a shaking hand at the floor. "It's Aspen, I think. She's dead."

Olive's frown deepened, and she stared at Beatrice as if she'd just said something very distasteful. "Of course she's not," she snapped. "I saw her just a few hours ago."

Olive strode up next to Beatrice and gasped when she looked at the floor. She started to step forward and Beatrice grabbed her arm. "We should leave it alone. The police will want to treat this as a crime scene."

Beatrice felt Olive stiffen.

"We need to talk to the conference administrators. That Starr, maybe," said Beatrice. "My paperwork is back at the cabin, though. It had her number on it."

Olive turned and walked to one of the sewing tables. She picked up several papers, scanning them with her eyes until she found a number. "I don't have my phone with me," she said.

Beatrice had grabbed hers on the way out of the cabin, concerned Piper might wake up and worry where she was. "What's the number?" she asked, pulling out the phone.

But to her frustration, her phone couldn't get a signal. Beatrice shoved it back in her pocket. She glanced around the room. "I don't see any landlines here."

Olive said, "That's hard to believe, considering the cell phone signal is poor here. I had a hard time using my phone yesterday, even before the weather got this bad."

"I wonder if I can get a text message through, instead. Although a text message might not wake up Starr like a phone call would."

Beatrice typed in a short message identifying herself and asking Starr if she was awake.

A few moments later, Starr answered the text with one of her own. "What's happened? What's wrong?"

"Aspen is dead. I found her a few minutes ago in the conference room," typed Beatrice. "I can't get a connection out to phone the police."

"Dead? She's the younger woman, isn't she? What happened?"

Beatrice took a deep breath to try to calm her erratic breathing. She typed: "She appears to have been stabbed."

Olive wrapped her arms around herself and stared at the body in front of her.

Starr typed, "Calling the police is the best thing to do, but I doubt they'll be able to come out today. I've been following the weather until I fell asleep a few minutes ago. There's a sheet of ice on the roads and they're closed. Emergency services have been suspended after an accident involving first responders."

Beatrice read Starr's text to Olive.

Olive said in an angry voice, "Somebody needs to take care of this. This is not what we signed up for when we came to the retreat. And where are the staff? They need to come over so that we're not the ones protecting the crime scene. Plus, there's a killer wandering around. That shouldn't be something we have to worry about."

Another text came in. "I'll try to contact the police from here. Just wait for me to arrive—I'll be there in a minute."

Beatrice put away her phone.

Olive said in a furious voice, "Why were you here in the middle of the night?"

Beatrice bristled, but tried to calm down. Olive was clearly upset by Aspen's death and seemed to be lashing out at everyone. "I couldn't sleep, so I thought some quiet quilting or reading might help me settle down and fall asleep. I didn't even know Aspen, and there was no reason for me to want to do her any harm. Why are *you* here?"

Olive tensed. "Same reason. I have a tough time sleeping in a new place. Plus, I saw lights on in here. I wondered what was going on."

Beatrice picked up the phone again and dialed 911. Again, there was no connection.

"Anything?" asked Olive tersely.

Beatrice shook her head. "There's no signal."

A text message dinged to indicate its arrival.

"It's Starr," said Beatrice, reading the message. "She says she was able to report Aspen's death, but the authorities are unable to make it here at this time."

"Surely the roads can't be that bad," said Olive. "Did they give Starr any sort of timeline?"

Beatrice typed the question and hit send. The response was almost immediate.

"Starr says the roads are closed because of icy conditions and that the police indicated there was more bad weather on the way. It could be a while." Beatrice paused. "I think we should just wait for Starr."

They waited silently, for what seemed like an hour. Olive paced, and Beatrice carefully avoided looking at the dead woman nearby.

"What's taking her so long?" snarled Olive.

Beatrice picked up the welcome packet Olive had been looking at and studied the map of the retreat. She said slowly, "It looks like there aren't any staff lodgings on site."

"What? You mean no one stays here overnight with the guests?"

Beatrice said, "Maybe that's why Starr made sure all the guests had her number in case of an emergency."

"How is she getting here then? She said the roads were all closed due to icy conditions."

Beatrice shrugged. "I'm not sure. Maybe she's just driving very slowly."

Olive was pacing again, and the sight of her walking back and forth was making Beatrice even more antsy.

Finally, the door pushed open and Starr stood there. The woman looked as though she was made from ice herself. Her winter clothing was covered with snow and ice and her face was red from the wind that was now gusting outside.

"Did you *walk* here?" asked Beatrice, stunned.

Starr nodded. "I don't live far away. It's impossible to drive a car and I don't have an ATV. This is unusual weather for here."

Olive said, "Well, clearly, Lakeside should have been cancelled this weekend. This is totally ridiculous."

Starr's face was stony, and she carefully ignored Olive's criticisms.

Olive continued, "What I want to know is what happened to Aspen. Plus, how are we going to have any amenities at the conference with no staff here? Do you have a plan for meals?"

Starr held up her hand to try to stem the flood of questions. "We have plenty of food here. I'll figure out a plan. First off, we need to leave this room. I'm going to lock it up."

"You're just going to leave Aspen like that?" Olive jutted her chin.

Starr said calmly, "I absolutely am. Otherwise, I'm interfering with a crime scene and you would be, too. We're leaving. Now."

"I don't want to go back to my cabin alone," said Olive.

Beatrice said, "You were rooming with Aspen?"

Olive nodded. "What if there's someone out there? I'll be by myself."

Starr frowned at her. "I seriously doubt someone is out in this storm, planning on picking off lone quilters. Besides, there are good locks on the cabin door."

"What if they simply break a window?"

Starr seemed on the brink of losing her patience. "Then someone will hear them. The cabins are close together. Now *out*."

Beatrice thought about suggesting that Olive could room with Miss Sissy, who was also by herself. She didn't really like the thought of Miss Sissy being alone with a killer on the loose, despite the old woman's fierceness. But for all she knew, Olive could be the murderer, herself. Instead, she'd just remind Miss Sissy to keep her door locked and secure.

"I'm not going to be staying here and quilting as if nothing has happened. There's a murderer here on the premises. I'm leaving the retreat today."

Starr shook her head, eyes steely. "You certainly aren't. The roads are closed. It would be a suicide mission if you tried. I was slipping and falling just *walking* over here from my home and it's close by. We're going to wait until conditions are better before anyone attempts to leave."

Olive seemed to bite back a sob and then quickly nodded.

Starr led Beatrice and Olive to another building. It appeared to be some sort of lodge. Beatrice hadn't gone in during the walk she took. Starr briskly unlocked the door, and they were greeted by a golden retriever who looked very excited to see them.

"This is Lucy. She's the retreat dog."

Beatrice reached out and Lucy nuzzled her. "She lives here?"

Starr nodded. "She stays in the lodge overnight." She walked in and turned on all the lights in the building. There was a large stone fireplace with leather recliners surrounding it. Beatrice remembered a picture of the room online.

Starr busied herself with making a fire. She seemed practiced at the chore and soon flames were licking around the wood.

Then Starr was on her phone. "I'll notify the group via email about the issue."

"About Aspen, you mean," muttered Olive.

Starr ignored her, still tapping her phone and frowning.

Beatrice said, "Are you able to get an internet connection? I couldn't, which is why I had to text. I could text with my data connection, but the connection wasn't strong enough to do anything else."

Starr shook her head, looking frustrated. "No. Wi-fi is touch and go here and now data is out, too. I'll try again later." She glanced over at Olive, who was sitting in one of the recliners, her hands raised to the fire. "Did you notice when Aspen left the cabin?"

"I wasn't her keeper," spat out Olive.

"There's no need to be defensive. I'm just trying to figure out what's going on."

Olive said in a low voice, "I remember hearing her leaving, but I just rolled over and tried to go back to sleep."

Starr asked, "Didn't you wonder where she was going in the middle of the night?"

"Not at all. Aspen is very independent." She paused. "*Was* very independent. If she wanted to go out for a walk, that wasn't any of my business. Besides, I was half asleep."

"A walk in this weather?" Starr's voice was skeptical.

"Why not? Clearly, Beatrice did and you're not asking her any questions."

Beatrice said, “I was having trouble sleeping, and I didn’t want to disturb my daughter in the next room. I remembered you said at the orientation that the conference room would be open twenty-four hours a day. I thought some quiet quilting or some reading might tire me out enough to get more sleep.” She held up her book which, fortunately, she’d had the presence of mind to bring with her.

Beatrice continued, “Since Aspen was in the conference room, she might have had trouble sleeping, too.”

Starr turned again to Olive. “You clearly realized at some point that Aspen was still outside.”

“Yes. I woke sometime later and remembered she’d gone. I peeked in the other room and she wasn’t there. I decided to get up and check on her. I didn’t look at the clock either time, so I have no idea when it was.”

“What did you make of Aspen?” asked Beatrice.

Olive shrugged, looking away. “I don’t know. We got along fairly well, under the circumstances.”

“What were the circumstances?” asked Starr.

“Aspen and I were ex-sisters-in-law. She’d been married for a while to my brother, Doug.”

Starr said slowly, “That must have been awkward. You being in a quilt guild with your brother’s ex.”

“It wasn’t awkward at all. The marriage simply didn’t work out. It happens all the time, doesn’t it? My own marriage has ups and downs, too. But that’s life, isn’t it? I’ve been very busy lately and my husband has been complaining that I’ve not been spending enough time with him.”

Beatrice asked, “Is it a job that’s keeping you so busy?”

Olive nodded. "I'm a math teacher. It's been a lot of grading lately and helping kids after school. Meetings, red tape, problems with administration, problems with students. It's like I've been dumped on all at once. That's the reason I'd been looking forward to this retreat so much. It was going to be a nice break from reality." Her mouth twisted ruefully.

"What did Aspen do for a living?" asked Starr.

Olive shrugged. "She was actually fairly mathematical, too. In her case, though, it was a different area of STEM. She was a programmer." She paused, looking somber. "This is going to come as quite a blow to Aspen's parents. They thought the world of her. I don't think I should tell them over the phone. That's the sort of news they should hear in person."

Beatrice said, "That's just as well, considering we've had such a tough time getting a cell phone signal."

Starr nodded. "I'm going to see if I can call the police again. Maybe I can get additional information or find out what they need for me to do." She stepped out of the room.

Olive rubbed her face, looking exhausted. "This is such a mess. I should have paid more attention to the weather forecast. This is not exactly the type of break I needed."

Beatrice was quiet for a few moments, hoping Olive would continue without prompting. Fortunately, she did. "Unfortunately, Aspen was really good at pushing people's buttons. I should have thought about that, too. If I had, I might have predicted that this wasn't going to be the stress-free weekend I was hoping for."

Beatrice asked, "Was there anyone in particular who Aspen was combative with?"

Olive gave a short laugh. "It was just about everybody. But I guess Ivy Fretwell was probably the one who was most unhappy."

Beatrice was going to ask her more about that when Starr returned to them, looking frustrated.

Chapter Six

"I was able to get a signal, but the phone rang and rang." Starr shrugged. "I guess they're swamped right now. Or maybe something's wrong with the phone line."

"There must be tons of accidents on the road, downed power lines, and medical calls," said Beatrice.

Olive shivered. "I simply can't believe this. Aspen was alive and well just a few hours ago."

Beatrice said, "It's got to be quite a shock."

"It's just hard to imagine that somebody was evil enough to do this."

Beatrice said, "You were saying that Ivy was probably the one who was most upset with Aspen."

"Aspen was having an affair with Ivy's husband." Olive gave a deep sigh. "It's just the kind of person she was." She said this in a very matter-of-fact tone.

Starr gave a low whistle. "Sounds like Aspen was really stirring things up. Did Ivy know about this?"

Olive nodded. "Ivy hadn't confronted Aspen about it yet, though. I got the feeling she was looking for a good opportunity. But it was pretty much an open secret in our town. Everybody knew about it."

Starr and Beatrice looked at each other.

"What if Ivy thought this was the perfect opportunity to finally confront Aspen?" asked Beatrice quietly.

Olive looked startled. "Here? I don't know."

"Seems like the perfect time to me," said Starr in a fake cheerful tone. "Maybe she confronted Aspen and her feelings got out of control. Maybe Aspen was snarky to her. And now we're stuck here with a body and a winter storm."

Olive shivered, whether because of the topic or the temperature. She said in a cranky tone, "I'm going to go put some warmer clothes on. The fire isn't even helping me feel warmer."

Beatrice said, "Do you need me to walk with you to the cabin?"

Olive briskly shook her head. "No, I think I'm okay now. I'm thinking a little more clearly."

"Before you go," said Beatrice quickly, "let's plan on keeping the details of Aspen's death quiet. No one should know but us that she was killed with a pair of shears."

"Good idea," said Starr quietly.

Olive gave a bob of her head in agreement and then quickly left the lodge. Starr rubbed her eyes. "This is all such a mess. Everybody's going to be up in a few hours, expecting food. And here I am with no cook."

"There's no way anyone can get over here, I guess?" asked Beatrice.

She shook her head. "Nope. Like I said, the only reason *I* was able to get here is because I live so close. I'm going to be the only staff member until the roads clear. And, from what I could see of the forecast, the temperatures will be far below freezing for days. And this is ice we're talking about, not just snow. It's especially treacherous."

Beatrice said, "One of the Village Quilters, Meadow, is an exceptional cook. I'm sure she'd be happy to help you out."

But Starr shook her head. "That's against retreat policy. I like to do everything by the book. Guests in the kitchen is a danger. The guest could get hurt or serve something others are allergic to . . . all sorts of things could happen that the retreat would ultimately be liable for. I'll handle the food."

That was disappointing. Beatrice was hoping at least they could have some good food while they were trapped there.

Starr frowned. "Another problem is keeping everyone occupied. All the guests planned on being here to quilt. I can't let anyone into the conference room to do that. No one probably brought other things to do."

Beatrice held up her book. "Some of us did."

"Yes, but I have the feeling most didn't." Starr paused, thinking. "I believe we have some other sewing machines in storage. I could set up an alternate space in the dining room."

Beatrice said, "The only problem with that is that many of us left our supplies in the conference room yesterday, preparing to quilt today."

Starr made a frustrated sound. "Right. I'll check and see if there are some notions in storage, too. And perhaps even some old fabric. We've been hosting these retreats for a long while; there might be plenty of things for people to do."

A grating voice behind them made them both jump. "S'moressss."

They whirled around to see Miss Sissy standing there. Her iron-gray hair was standing up on the top of her head like the bride of Frankenstein's monster. She was glowering at the both of them.

Starr quickly pasted a professional smile on her face. "Yes, s'mores were mentioned, weren't they? The only problem is the weather."

Miss Sissy didn't seem to comprehend how the snow and ice might prevent s'mores from happening. She snarled at Starr.

"Maybe we can make them over the fireplace later," said Beatrice.

Miss Sissy nodded eagerly, looking over at the fireplace. She walked closer so that she could feel the warmth. "Breakfast," she muttered.

Starr rubbed her face. "I hardly know what to start doing first. Look for fabric and put sewing machines in the dining room? Try the police again? Make breakfast?"

"Making breakfast might be the best idea," said Beatrice. "Everyone will be up soon. Serving food will be a good way to keep everyone happy."

Miss Sissy growled again in agreement.

Starr quickly left, glancing back at Miss Sissy as she walked out. As she was looking back, she nearly ran into Meadow. Starr murmured an apology and kept going.

"What's going on?" asked Meadow. "I tried to drop off some more supplies in the conference room and it was locked tight. I thought they said the room was supposed to be open twenty-four hours a day."

Miss Sissy gave an exasperated grunt at this, as if not at all surprised that things were running so poorly at the retreat.

Beatrice sighed. "There's been an incident."

Meadow put her hands on her hips. "What sort of incident? Don't tell me there's something wrong with the sewing machines or something. That would really be ridiculous."

"Do you remember Aspen yesterday?"

Meadow snorted. "Of course I do. She stood out, didn't she? She wasn't particularly behaving herself. I expect a higher standard from quilters. But she seemed like the sort of person who might stir up trouble."

"In some ways, I guess she did. But the trouble was for her this time. Someone murdered her last night."

Meadow gaped at her. "No! Here at the retreat?"

Her voice intimated that retreats were not intended to be places where murderers were running around willy nilly. Beatrice said, "I'm afraid so. I discovered her a couple of hours ago."

Miss Sissy scowled at this. "Evilllllll."

"Yes," agreed Beatrice.

Meadow's hands were still on her hips. "So someone sneaked into our quilting retreat and decided to kill one of the quilters?"

Beatrice shook her head. "I don't think that's what happened. There's another factor—the weather. The roads have all been closed. Not even emergency vehicles can get through. This appears to have been an inside job."

"You're saying someone from the *retreat* did this?" asked Meadow.

Beatrice nodded.

Meadow spluttered and found herself quite speechless for a few moments.

Miss Sissy intoned, "*Evillll!*" once again.

"What are we going to do now?" asked Meadow. "Are we just leaving that poor girl where you found her? And where exactly *did* you find her?"

Beatrice said, "In the conference room. That's why you couldn't get in there. When I couldn't sleep, I thought I could get some work done and that might make me sleepy. But instead, I found Aspen in there."

"You're sure it wasn't just a natural death?"

Beatrice nodded. "I'm afraid not."

Meadow shuddered. "Got it." She frowned. "So we won't be able to get into that room for the duration, I guess."

"Starr locked it up."

"And you've called the police?" asked Meadow.

"Well, that's been something of a problem. Our cell phones don't seem to work well here. I was able to text Starr and she could report the problem, but because of the weather, it looks like it might be a while before anyone is able to get here."

Miss Sissy snarled. Whether it was at the lateness of emergency services or the world in general was unclear.

Meadow said, "Well, if I'm going to entertain myself today, I guess I better head back to the cabin and get more things out."

Beatrice said, "At least you have more projects to work on. I brought everything over to the conference room, and I think Piper did, too. Starr was going to check and see if she could find a fabric stash. I do have my book to read, luckily."

"Oh, I've got a pile of projects, and I wasn't organized enough yesterday to sort them all out. That seems lucky, now. If you need something, I've probably got some stuff you could work on."

Beatrice gave a short laugh. "I might take you up on that, depending on how long we're stuck here." She paused. "I wonder if I could at least help myself to a bowl of cereal in the dining hall. No cooking required, after all. Surely there are continental breakfast options there. I've been up for a while."

Miss Sissy, who had *not* been up for a while, perked up at the mention of food.

"Let's head out, then," said Meadow. "I'll run by the cabin first and will meet you in a few minutes."

It was precisely the "running by the cabin" bit that became problematic for Meadow. In her haste, she set out onto the icy path and made a wild slipping dance, yelping loudly all the way. Beatrice slid down the path toward her to try to help but was soon yelping and sliding, herself. Miss Sissy glowered at them for a few moments before resolutely stomping in the direction of the dining hall.

Meadow and Beatrice finally regained their balance and stood there panting for a bit to catch their breaths and wait for their hearts to stop pounding so hard.

A voice hissed at them. "What is going on?"

It was a well-preserved and elegant woman. She seemed very annoyed at the commotion they'd caused. Although she'd apparently been awakened, she still somehow retained a very well put-together look.

"Have you been drinking?" asked the woman, suspiciously.

"Drinking?" asked Beatrice with a snort. "We've not had a drop. We're simply trying to walk. Take a few steps."

Still looking very suspicious, the woman did. One foot promptly slid out in front of her and she drew it back in quickly. "I see," she muttered.

Another woman joined them. She looked like an older version of the first woman. She said, "Why don't you go back to the cabin, Maggie? Get a little sleep. I'm just going to pop out and get some breakfast."

Maggie grunted and then said, "I suppose I could try. Although now I'm feeling quite awake." She shot Meadow and Beatrice an annoyed look and slid away.

The other woman grimaced and gave them a small smile. "Sorry about my sister. I'm Nicole, by the way. Anyway, Maggie's ordinarily not like that. She definitely needs to get more sleep. She's had some stressful stuff go on lately."

Meadow gave her an understanding look as they took small steps in the direction of the dining hall. "Quilting is a wonderful stress-reliever, isn't it? Of course she wanted to come to the retreat and work on a quilt."

Nicole said, "Well, that was the idea. I'm afraid the weather is keeping it from being quite as relaxing as it should be."

Beatrice just hoped the power stayed on. It didn't take much ice at all to bring down power lines. There was definitely a good coating on the ground. She decided not to say anything to the others but keep her worries to herself.

Meadow glanced at Nicole and said slowly, "Well, there's another problem with the retreat. Besides the weather, I mean." She looked over at Beatrice.

Beatrice said, "I'm afraid there's been an incident." She hesitated. "Were you very close to Aspen?"

Nicole gave a short laugh. "I don't think anybody is really close to Aspen. An incident? What's she done now? Are the Sew and Sews kicked out of the retreat because of something she did?"

"No, it's nothing like that. I'm sorry, but Aspen is dead."

Nicole stopped short as they finally entered the dining hall, staring at them. "What? What do you mean? Did she slip on the ice and crack her head?"

Meadow said, "Nicole, it's awful. Aspen was murdered last night."

Nicole swayed a little unsteadily, despite not being on icy ground any longer.

Beatrice said, "Let's get you inside."

As Meadow and Beatrice ushered Nicole in, Starr looked cross. "I'm really not ready—" she started. Then, seeing the shocked look on Nicole's face, she hurried over. "Are you all right?"

"She just heard the news about Aspen," said Beatrice.

They settled Nicole into one of the seats in the dining hall, and Starr hurried off to get some water.

"Murdered," breathed Nicole.

Starr slid the water in front of her just moments later. Her face was puckered with concern. Speaking almost to herself, she said, "This isn't good. I'll need to make an announcement. But I still don't have a connection to send a group email. I'll plan for a meeting with everyone in the dining hall and announce it over our intercom system."

Meadow chirped up, "If you're wanting to announce what happened to Aspen, you'll need to plan that in advance. You can't cook at the same time. I could take over the cooking."

Starr looked momentarily annoyed before seeming to give the offer serious thought. "I guess these are emergency conditions," she said grudgingly. "I already had to stop what I was doing to feed your friend."

And indeed, Miss Sissy, through sheer will, had gotten Starr to drop everything and make her toast.

"She's an excellent cook," Beatrice reiterated.

Starr nodded. "Okay. I did review all the guest paperwork in my office, and no one reported any food allergies."

Meadow scampered off to the kitchen. She was never happier than when she was cooking, playing with her grandson, or quilting.

Nicole gave a somewhat hysterical laugh, making Beatrice and Starr look at her with concern. She said, "Aspen always *could* cause a lot of commotion. This is par for the course."

"What kind of commotion did she usually cause?" asked Beatrice. She noticed with relief that Nicole seemed to be recovering her equanimity.

"Oh, I'd say she specialized in general mischief. Aspen could be passive aggressive and, if she was bored enough, she was actively aggressive."

"Any particular examples of general mischief?" asked Starr.

Nicole's gaze sharpened. "You're trying to find suspects, aren't you?"

Beatrice said, “Unfortunately, the police don’t seem to be coming anytime soon. I’m just trying to collect information so that we can understand what’s going on.”

Nicole put her hands up in a reflexively defensive posture. “I had nothing to do with it. I was asleep and so was my sister, Maggie. Both of us slept hard until we heard all the ruckus outside.”

“Ruckus?” frowned Starr.

Nicole gestured to Beatrice. “She and her friend were outside trying to walk and not doing a very good job at it.”

Starr frowned again. “Getting everyone over to the auditorium might be too hard. Perhaps the dining hall would be a better place for me to announce what’s happened.”

Nicole’s eyes narrowed. “What sort of business are you running here? Are we thinking someone came on the premises and murdered a guest in cold blood?”

“I’m not thinking that at all,” said Starr in a calm but irritated voice. “Like you mentioned before, I’m trying to find suspects among the Sew and Sews group. The Village Quilters didn’t even know her. Plus, there’s a dangerous winter storm outside and also nothing of real, marketable value in the conference room. So no, I don’t think anyone slipped onto the retreat grounds and murdered your friend.”

“She wasn’t *my* friend,” muttered Nicole.

Meadow came back over with mugs of steaming coffee on a platter. She set the platter down and said, “Luckily, we have Beatrice here. She’s a wonderful amateur sleuth.”

Beatrice colored a little as both Nicole and Starr turned to look at her. “I wouldn’t say I’m a sleuth.”

"Of *course* you are!" Meadow said. She turned to the other women and said, "She helps out my husband all the time on his cases. And he's the police chief in our town."

After dropping this bit of information, she scurried off again toward the kitchen.

Chapter Seven

Beatrice cleared her throat, feeling awkward. "I'm no professional, by any means. But I have time on my hands and my husband is a minister, so people tend to talk to me about their concerns. I agree with you, Starr. I can't imagine anyone venturing out in this weather unless they actually knew there was something of real value, something they could fence, on the premises. How would they even know if they could get away from the retreat center afterwards to make their getaway? The ice out there is immobilizing."

Nicole put her face in her hands. "So it's one of the group."

Starr said, "Like I was saying, it's likely not one of the Village Quilters."

Meadow, who apparently still had excellent hearing, called from the kitchen, "Of *course* not! The Village Quilters would never consider doing such a thing."

"Just as good as gold, are you?" asked Nicole with a snort.

Beatrice said, "To be fair, we don't know any of you. We're from a different town."

"Maybe one of you knew Aspen earlier in her life or something," said Nicole.

Beatrice ignored this. "What did you make of Aspen?"

Nicole grew still and considered her answer. "We got along fine. I tried to stay out of her way as much as possible, which definitely helped."

"And your sister? Maggie?"

Nicole shrugged, looking down at the table. "The same. She and I never socialized with Aspen at any of the guild meetings or events. We thought of her as someone to steer clear of, like I said. It seemed like the best way to prevent any trouble."

Beatrice said, "What sort of quilter was Aspen? It seems to me like too much of a quiet activity for someone like her."

"She was a great quilter, actually. Had a great eye, was talented, creative, and practiced. It was something she'd been doing most of her life. I remember one time she said that she found it soothing." Nicole paused. "I was surprised she was a quilter, too. I thought that she was too abrasive a personality to really excel that way. I wonder if sometimes she took out her aggression on the quilts. I wasn't a fan of some of her experimental quilts. Too wild and crazy for me."

Starr said, "Who do you think might have done something like this?"

"Nobody," said Nicole stubbornly.

"Okay then, who do you think most disliked Aspen? From the Sew and Sews," pushed Starr.

Nicole once again took a few moments to consider the question.

"I'm not saying this woman had anything to do with what happened. Got it?"

Starr and Beatrice nodded.

Apparently satisfied, Nicole continued. "Cora Turner didn't like Aspen one bit. I'm not sure exactly what the problem between the two of them was. But you could just feel the waves of irritation and dislike coming off her."

Starr jotted this down in a small notebook. "And Cora is here on the retreat?"

"She is. She never would have come if she'd known Aspen was coming. At first, it looked as if Aspen had a conflict or wasn't going to be able to make it. I guess she must have rearranged her schedule at the last minute."

Starr nodded. Then she looked around as if thinking of a million different things she needed to do. She said slowly, "I'm glad Meadow is helping out in the kitchen, even if it's against policy. To make this work better, though, it would be good to get prep-work done for supper tonight. Slicing up vegetables and that kind of thing."

It was definitely a leading statement. Nicole quickly said, "I'm out. I'm not interested in helping set up the kitchen. I'm heading back to bed."

"There's food being prepared," Beatrice pointed out.

"I'll get leftovers later. I paid for a certain experience here at the retreat, and it's not being delivered. I'll be asking for a refund after we get out of here."

With that, Nicole stomped off. Starr watched her, looking deflated.

"We'll help out," said Beatrice quickly. "Meadow would be delighted to, I'm sure, after she finishes preparing breakfast. I'm not great in a kitchen, but I can definitely slice vegetables. I'm sure most of the Village Quilters would be happy to lend a hand."

Starr gave her a relieved look. "That would be great." She paused. "I know this isn't what you signed up for."

"It's not as if there's a lot else to do."

Starr said, "Okay. I'm heading to my office to try the police again. Then I'll come up with a short statement to say what happened and how we can make this all work."

Beatrice quirked a brow. "How *are* we going to make this all work?"

Starr gave her a wry smile. "That's what I've got to figure out. I'll duck back into the lodge for a few minutes—my office is in that building."

"I'm just glad you're here," said Beatrice. "It would be awful if we were left to our own devices." She paused. "You're not the owner of the retreat, are you? I'm not sure I got your background." She also wasn't sure if she simply hadn't been paying attention when Starr introduced herself at the orientation. Things changed with the advent of winter weather. And with a dead body.

Starr was shaking her head. "The owner lives on the other side of the country and handles everything remotely. I've been the manager here for a long time. I guess I feel a lot of responsibility for the conference center. Besides, like I mentioned, I live nearby." She hurried out of the door to the lodge.

Meadow came out of the kitchen with a stack of pancakes and a bottle of syrup. "What happened to everybody?"

"Starr went to her office and Nicole left to go back to lie down."

Miss Sissy spotted the pancakes and scampered over to their table.

"Didn't you just eat, Miss Sissy?" asked Meadow in a jolly tone. "Well, I guess it won't hurt for you to have a few more. I'll eat along with y'all. Before the morning rush comes in."

They took plates and heaped them with pancakes.

Meadow said thoughtfully. "Starr is devoted to her job, I guess."

"A good thing, considering we're the beneficiaries of that." Beatrice paused. "Did you ever work outside the home? I don't think I've ever asked you that." Or if she did, she'd forgotten Meadow's answer.

Meadow said, "Oh, sure I did. Off and on, you know. I wasn't exactly a bank executive, but I pulled in a bit of extra income from time to time before we had Ash and then after he was in school." A mischievous look came over her face. "Guess what I did."

Beatrice considered this. "You worked at a plant nursery."

Meadow's face fell. "How did you guess?"

"You're great with plants and always have that veggie garden. It made sense. It was either that or you might have worked at that funky boutique that's downtown."

Meadow blinked. "Hey, you *are* good. I've always thought about working there. I'd have gotten a discount and I love their clothes."

Miss Sissy shot them both an annoyed look as if they were purposefully distracting her from her devouring of the pancakes.

Meadow gave the old woman an indulgent look. "Miss Sissy, did you ever have a job?"

Miss Sissy gave a ferocious snarl and continued her demolition of the pancakes.

Realizing she wasn't going to get an answer, Meadow moved onto other musings. "I suppose now that it's a good thing I didn't bring Cammie to the retreat."

"You were planning to bring a dog to a quilting retreat?" asked Beatrice.

"Well, I wouldn't have brought Boris, of course. You know I love the big goof, but there's no way I'd be able to smuggle him in. Or, I suppose, smuggle him in and out of the cabin to potty."

Beatrice said, "But you were going to do that with Cammie?"

"Well, she's tiny! I thought it might be sort of fun to have her here. She's grown very fond of me. Plus, it's been so recent since she lost her other human mommy. I was worried she might imagine something awful had happened to me while I was gone, even though she loves Ramsay."

Miss Sissy snorted at this.

Meadow continued, "But then I started thinking about how jealous Boris would be if I took Cammie and didn't take him. And Cammie is so prissy she'd never have wanted to go outside and use the bathroom in this horrid ice and snow. Just as well that I didn't bring her."

Beatrice had no illusions why Boris wouldn't be suitable for the quilting retreat. He was a holy terror most of the time. He wasn't good on a leash, would likely have barked at the falling snow, and was a voracious eater who had no qualms about grabbing and gobbling food from countertops and tables. Noo-noo, on the other hand, would have been perfectly behaved. Beatrice felt a little stab, missing her sweet corgi. Maybe it was because of the shock of finding Aspen, but she felt she could use the comforting little dog.

She pulled out her phone. "I'm going to try to get a connection again. Wyatt is probably getting concerned about the winter storm trapping us." She tried dialing out and shook her head. "Still no connection."

She tapped out a text message and tried sending it. It had worked when she contacted Starr, but didn't now. "I can't text now either."

Meadow looked a little panicky and tried her phone, which was also dead. "Oh no. I'd planned on checking in with Ramsay."

"And tell him about the murder?" asked Beatrice.

"What? No. I wanted to see how our grandbaby is doing. Ramsay was supposed to be watching Will today for Ash, and I was going to ask for pictures."

Beatrice said, "The ice storm might have derailed those plans."

Meadow sighed. "I'll just try again later."

Olive joined them again, now wearing the warmer clothes she'd set out for. She frowned. "I wasn't able to call out on my phone a few minutes ago."

"We just tried with no luck," said Meadow, sounding a little wound up.

Olive sighed. "I thought it might have been just a momentary disruption to the network, but it's looking like something more serious." She paused. "I saw Nicole on her way to her cabin. Did you speak with her?"

Beatrice nodded. "She seemed out of sorts. Not surprising, I suppose, especially considering the circumstances."

"I don't know what's been eating her lately," said Olive. "She's been so overprotective of Maggie. I mean, of *course* you want to look out for your sister, but it seems over the top recently. I've been wondering if maybe Maggie was dealing with some sort of health crisis or something. Maybe that would trigger her reaction."

"Has Maggie seemed sick?" asked Meadow.

Olive shook her head. "Not that I can see. But she could still be dealing with something privately."

"Would you like some pancakes? I've whipped up a big batch of batter," said Meadow.

Olive smiled at her. "Actually, that would be fantastic. I've been up for a while now and my stomach is about to start growling."

"More for you, Beatrice?" asked Meadow.

"Oh, no. No, I'm good. They were delicious, but if I have any more carbs, I'm going to have to go straight back to bed." She paused. "I wish the police would get here. Somebody needs to get to the bottom of this."

"I'll say," said Olive with a sniff. "If nothing else, it's a risk to *us* having a killer on the loose."

Meadow, who'd stood up to get back on pancake duty, said stoutly, "Well, in lieu of police help, I nominate Beatrice to dig things up. She's a gifted amateur. Beatrice could poke around and try to figure out why someone might have wanted to get rid of Aspen."

Olive raised her eyebrows. "It's not a horrible idea. We could be here for an extended period. There's no sun and these temperatures aren't going to be melting anything anytime soon."

Meadow said, "Olive, you were rooming with Aspen. Did she bring any personal items with her? A journal, or a notebook, or a laptop, or something? Maybe Beatrice can find some clues to figure out who might have done this."

Beatrice demurred. "I'm not sure that's something I should do. After all, the police are going to want to look her personal effects as soon as they get here."

"Which might be *ages*," said Meadow. "You don't need to mess anything up—just take a brief look and see what you can find out." She turned again to Olive and repeated impatiently, "So—a journal?"

"She wasn't exactly the sort of introspective person who might keep a journal," said Olive with a twist of her lips. "But I did glimpse a computer. Won't it need a password to get in, though?"

"It might. I could give it a try, though. If it does have a password, do you have any idea what it might be?" asked Beatrice.

Olive snorted. "Nope. I have no idea what Aspen might have thought a good password. And because she was in IT, I'm imagining it might have been a secure one."

"Would you mind if I take a look at it? Go into your cabin?"

Olive made a shooing gesture at her. "Knock yourself out. The sooner we figure out what's going on, the safer I'll feel."

Beatrice nodded. "Okay. I'll put on my winter gloves so I won't disturb any fingerprints or anything."

Beatrice pulled her gloves out of the pocket of her heavy coat. They were fluffy and very warm—a present from Wyatt from last Christmas.

Olive looked at them with disbelief. "Those gloves are huge! You won't be able to type in those things. Here, take mine."

She handed Beatrice a pair of slim, brown leather gloves that fit Beatrice's fingers perfectly.

"Thanks," said Beatrice.

Olive again waved her off, after giving her a key to the cabin.

The cabin was designed very much like the one Beatrice and Piper shared. Two bedrooms, two small bathrooms, and a kitchenette/sitting area.

One bedroom immediately seemed to be Olive's. Beatrice could see a lot of unimaginative clothing hanging neatly in the closet. The bed was made, and everything seemed very tidy.

The other room was clearly Aspen's. It was messier, with makeup items strewn across the room. A bottle of vodka was visible on the bedside table and there was clothing on the floor and the bed.

Looking closer, Beatrice spotted the laptop Olive had mentioned. Holding her breath, Beatrice opened it and waited to see if it would prompt her for a password. It did.

Beatrice sighed. She certainly didn't know Aspen well enough to be able to guess a password for her. And, since Aspen was a computer professional, it seemed like she'd have something pretty secure for her laptop.

Beatrice thought about it for a minute. She thought the young woman seemed cocky enough to put in something really simple. And she appeared to have been a fairly self-centered individual. She hesitantly put in *Aspen* and the computer sprang to life.

Chapter Eight

But Beatrice wasn't completely sure what she was looking at. On her own computer, her homepage was Google. But this looked like a completely different browser altogether. And not one of the three she was familiar with. It was something called Tor.

Beatrice also noticed that there was no online connection to the browser and sighed. She'd hoped that perhaps she could send an email to Wyatt later to explain what had happened, but it looked like that definitely wasn't going to be the case.

Hesitantly, she looked at the bookmarks that Aspen had saved. This puzzled her again, because instead of ending in .com or .org, the sites ended in .onion.

"What on earth?" muttered Beatrice under her breath. She took a few pictures with her phone, and then carefully closed the laptop again.

Beatrice ventured back outside. The weather, if anything, had gotten worse. Ice was spitting out of the sky and gales of wind were slinging it into her face. What was worse was the fact that she couldn't hurry, or she'd slip on the treacherous ice under her feet. When she reached the dining hall, she looked into the room for Olive, but didn't see her there. She saw that many of the quilters were now up and being fed by Meadow.

Beatrice tried the lodge next. There were only so many places Olive could be, considering she'd just been in her cabin and the conference room was closed off.

She finally found her in front of a roaring fire in the lodge, looking a bit drowsy and absently petting Lucy, the golden retriever. Lucy seemed to be enjoying the attention and was practically grinning.

"Just wanted to bring key back to you. Oh, and your gloves," said Beatrice. "You'll need them out there."

Olive nodded curtly, then studied Beatrice's features. "You found something." Her voice was flat but certain.

Beatrice said slowly, "I did, but I'm not exactly sure what it is that I *did* find."

"What do you mean?" Her gaze was piercing.

Beatrice showed her some of the pictures she'd taken with her phone. "I wasn't sure what all this was."

Olive frowned, eyes narrowed, as she scrolled through the photos. "I see."

"What do you see?"

Olive handed the phone back to Beatrice. In that same flat voice she said, "The dark web." Her brows knit together as she considered the implications of that.

Beatrice's eyes widened. "You think Aspen was involved with illegal activity?"

Olive gave a short laugh. "Most likely. You only get there with a special web browser, so it's not like she just happened upon it while she was shopping online."

"The only thing I know about the dark web is that a lot of stolen credit card numbers end up for sale there. And stolen identities."

Olive nodded. "There's more to it than that, of course. I don't know a lot about it myself, but I've read you can buy and sell weapons, drugs, passwords, and other illegal things. I can't say I'm surprised. Aspen was the type of person who would get into that sort of thing. Plus, she was very computer-savvy."

"It sounds like you're pretty computer-savvy, yourself," said Beatrice.

Olive shrugged. "Somewhat. Like I said, I'm a math teacher. I've dabbled in some programming and have an interest in IT." She glanced toward the door leading from the lodge. "Ugh, it looks like Ivy is coming in. I just don't have the patience for her nonsense right now."

With that, she abruptly stood up, clasping the leather gloves, and swept out of the lodge through a different door. Lucy, the golden retriever, sadly watched her go. Beatrice reached out and scratched Lucy behind her ears and the dog gave her a grateful look.

Beatrice remembered Olive had mentioned that Aspen had been having an affair with Ivy's husband.

A few moments later, a woman in her late-forties came in. She looked tired and cross. Beatrice could tell that she must have been a great beauty in earlier years, although that beauty was somewhat faded now.

"This place is the worst," she muttered to Beatrice, sitting next to her in one of the armchairs facing the fire. "Their stupid PA system woke me up with a meeting announcement. Who has a meeting at this time of the morning?"

Beatrice glanced at her watch. It was after nine o'clock now.

The golden retriever looked askance at Ivy, worried about her irritated tone.

Perhaps sensing a lack of sympathy from Beatrice, Ivy sniffed. "It's vacation time. The last thing I want to think about is a stupid meeting."

Ivy tinkered with her cell phone for a few moments before dropping it into her lap. "At least we could have better wi-fi. I can't get through to anybody."

Beatrice decided that Ivy was apparently not the most observant person. "That's actually due to the weather outside. The ice you walked through."

Ivy's pretty face furrowed with annoyance. "That's another thing. I tend to expect better customer service when I travel. You'd think the staff could at least have shoveled the walkways. They're going to be sued up one side and down another if anyone falls and breaks something."

"You can't really shovel ice," noted Beatrice. "And there *isn't* any staff here, aside from the manager, who walked from her home. The roads are all closed because they're too hazardous to drive on."

Ivy was determined to rant about the management. "Then they should never have allowed us to be here in the first place."

That was something Beatrice could agree with, despite the fact that no one had really seen this weather coming. Still, she supposed the retreat could have closed out of an abundance of caution.

Ivy huffed, "Maybe they're holding the meeting to say they're going to refund us our money because of all the inconveniences."

Beatrice shook her head. "The meeting is on a slightly more serious topic."

"There's nothing more serious than poor customer service." Ivy pressed her lips together.

Beatrice thought she knew the answer to the question she was about to ask, but she wanted to see Ivy's reaction. "Are you close to Aspen?"

Ivy blinked at her as if the words didn't compute. "Close to *Aspen*? You mean geographically? Or emotionally?"

"As a friend."

Ivy spluttered into a laugh. "No, of course not. Aspen is a thoroughly unpleasant woman. No one is close to Aspen." She paused. "Don't tell me she took off and left for home before the weather got bad. Deserting us is just the type of thing I'd expect from her. We'll all probably be getting text messages with pictures of Aspen curled up at home drinking wine while we're trying to manage third-world problems at this so-called retreat."

Beatrice decided she'd gotten a bit more feedback on Aspen than she'd planned for. At least it was very clear what Ivy's feelings about Aspen were.

"So you didn't see Aspen late last night?"

Now Ivy was looking cranky. "What's with all the questions? Is Aspen missing? I don't think she wandered off into the snow and ice. Taking walks or communing with nature isn't what Aspen is all about. Like I said, she most likely drove off and abandoned her fellow guild members. She drives an all-wheel drive . . . a tricked-out Jeep. Well, that's *one* of her cars, anyway, and it's the one she brought here. She left us, I'm sure of it. And I, for one, am delighted to hear she did, even if I do get an obnoxious, gloating text message later." She paused, seeing Beatrice still looking searchingly at her. "But to answer your question, no.

No, I didn't see Aspen last night or this morning. I turned in early and just got up. I slept like the dead."

Beatrice said, "The reason I was asking is that I was trying to figure out what might have happened. Aspen is dead. She was murdered last night."

Ivy's eyes opened wide in astonishment. Then Beatrice thought she saw the slightest hint of unholy glee. "You're kidding."

Now Beatrice was the one who felt cranky. "Of course not. Who would joke about something like that?"

"Dead? Aspen? But how? Where?" Ivy started looking around her as if Aspen's body might pop out from behind an armchair or from around a wall.

Beatrice again realized some of the details might best be kept quiet. After all, it was a police strategy to divulge as little information as possible. Only she, Starr, and Olive had seen Aspen. She said, "She's in the conference room that was set up for quilting. The room's been locked up now."

This appeared to peeve Ivy even further. "No *quilting*? But that's the entire reason we're here. Of *course* Aspen managed to mess that up." She looked at Beatrice with narrowed eyes. "What happened to her?"

"We don't really know. That's up to the police to decide."

Ivy pressed on. "But you said she was murdered."

"It's a suspicious death."

Ivy now seemed to be in a much better humor than she was previously. "So the meeting is about the murder?"

Beatrice nodded.

Suddenly, Ivy's face fell again. "But wait! That means we're here with a killer loose. Where are the police? Why aren't we all being rescued?"

Beatrice wasn't sure if Ivy was a little slow on the uptake or whether she was simply so self-centered that she couldn't think beyond her own needs. "Because the police can't get here. The roads are too dangerous. The rescuers would end up needing to be rescued themselves."

This was apparently a most unsatisfactory response. Ivy glared at Beatrice as if the whole thing were her fault.

"What about security? Isn't this manager or whoever she is, going to call in some staff to handle this? Is she the only one who lives close-by?"

Beatrice nodded.

Ivy's breath hissed out of her. "It was probably some drifter trying to get away from the storm. The conference room was open all day and all night . . . that's what the staff had said yesterday at the orientation. Anybody could have walked in to get warm. Then, when Aspen surprised them, they killed her." She looked at Beatrice. "That's it. That's what happened."

"That *could* have happened," acknowledged Beatrice.

"But you obviously don't think it did." Ivy threw a petulant look at her, disliking being crossed.

"Considering what I've heard about Aspen, it sounds likely that someone might have harbored ill-will towards her."

"Is that your polite way of saying no one liked her? Because I agree with you. She was a horrible human being." Ivy sounded grimly satisfied that Aspen was no longer a problem.

Beatrice said, "Someone mentioned that you might have had reason to dislike Aspen, too."

Ivy's eyes filled with malice. "Who said that? If there's one thing I can't abide is gossipy women."

"Is it true?"

Ivy looked away. "My husband is a good husband. A good provider, too. He cares about me. But I guess Aspen stumbled across one of his few weaknesses. He couldn't resist the silly woman." Her gaze sharpened again as she looked back at Beatrice. "No one was suggesting I had anything to do with Aspen's death, were they? What a horrid thing to say! I've been nothing but law-abiding my entire life. An excellent citizen in every way. I volunteered with the Junior League for ages before I became a sustainer. I had no involvement with her murder."

Beatrice nodded.

Ivy added, "But I'd like to give an award to whoever did."

Beatrice had never really met someone as venomous as Ivy. It made her want to be back in Dappled Hills with Wyatt. Somehow, Wyatt always seemed to see the good side of everyone. It was a quality that made him such an excellent minister. Ivy, on the other hand, made Beatrice feel almost tainted by association. No wonder Olive hadn't wanted to stick around and talk to Ivy.

"I still feel it must be some sort of drifter who did this. But I do know someone else who wasn't crazy about Aspen. Olive. Olive and I have had many long talks about Aspen. She married Olive's brother, Doug, and treated him horribly."

"In what way?"

"In *every* way. The poor sap was clearly crazy about her and she acted as if she could take him or leave him. She spoke very condescendingly towards Doug, almost as if she didn't have a whit of respect for him. Then she kept cheating on him." She lowered her voice dramatically, looking around to make sure no one was listening. "In fact, Doug took his own life."

Beatrice shook her head. "That's awful," she said quietly. Olive hadn't gone into any detail about Doug and Aspen. Perhaps it was a topic that was too painful for her to discuss.

"It's truly awful, yes. Doug found out Aspen had been cheating on him and was planning on leaving him. Olive has blamed Aspen for it, and rightfully so. Olive and Doug were very close."

The golden retriever bumped her head against Beatrice's leg, and she absently reached down to rub Lucy. "It must have been very awkward, having Aspen in the same quilting guild."

Ivy snorted. "Maybe it was awkward for Olive, but it didn't seem to bother Aspen one whit. She was delighted at all the trouble and angst she was causing. She was never happier than when she was making everyone talk about her. She loved the attention. Reveled in it."

Beatrice thought back to Aspen's computer and what she'd seen inside. "Do you know anything about the dark web?"

Ivy stared at her as if she'd suddenly grown two horns. "The what?"

"Never mind. It's just something I was wondering about."

Ivy picked up her phone again, punching buttons and frowning. She held the phone up to her ear. "Ridiculous."

"No signal still?"

"None at all!" said Ivy. "Which would be okay if we actually had wi-fi. My husband is going to be worried about me. I need to let him know what's going on." She paused. "Maybe he can come and pick me up. He has a Jeep."

Beatrice shook her head. "That's not going to help when it comes to driving on a sheet of ice. Not on these mountain roads, especially. You wouldn't want anything to happen to him."

Ivy's mouth curved down in displeasure. "It just stinks being in this situation to begin with. I don't feel safe at all with the lack of staff and a killer running around."

"I'll say!" said a voice behind them.

The two women turned to see Meadow coming into the lodge.

Beatrice introduced Ivy to Meadow. Meadow gave Ivy a big, friendly smile, and Ivy pressed her lips together and nodded.

"Finally finished with your kitchen duty?" asked Beatrice.

"Yes, thank goodness. I like cooking, but people kept coming into the kitchen to help, and it was driving me crazy. One woman would walk off with a measuring cup and another had the butter. I finally just kicked everyone out."

"You work here?" asked Ivy, looking as if she were about to launch into a litany of criticisms.

Meadow gave her a cheerful smile. "Nope! But I've volunteered to help out in the kitchen."

"Which we're very grateful for," added Beatrice. "The expression on Starr's face when she realized she would have to take over the cooking led me to believe she's not much of a cook."

"I wonder how much food is on hand?" asked Ivy.

Beatrice held back a smile. It looked as if Ivy's imagination might be running away from her. A winter storm and then lack of food? "I'm sure we're in good shape. Don't you think so, Meadow?"

"From what I could see. They have an industrial-size fridge, for sure. The pantry looked huge and well-stocked."

The door opened again, sending in another blast of arctic air. Starr came in, wearing even more winter gear than she had the first time Beatrice saw her. She strode up to the fire, rubbing her hands together. Lucy, the retriever, nuzzled at her leg and Starr reached down to give the dog a loving rub.

Ivy's eyes narrowed. "You're in charge here?"

"That's right," said Starr with a tight smile. "You didn't make it to the meeting I held?"

Ivy shrugged. "I thought it was going to be something stupid. Could you give me a recap?"

"Considering that was the whole point of the meeting, I'll let someone else fill you in. I don't feel like repeating myself. I have other things to worry about."

"Like food?" asked Ivy with trepidation, still thinking about her worst-case-scenario.

"No, like making sure everyone stays safe and warm. Food isn't going to be a problem."

Ivy visibly relaxed into her armchair.

Meadow fretted, "I wish I could let Ramsay know about the issues here. He would come over here and sort things out."

Starr shook her head. "It's too dangerous for anyone to risk driving here."

"Even on an ATV?"

Starr said, "An ATV would be better, but I'd think it would still struggle."

Beatrice said, "Plus, it's so far away, Meadow. We drove ninety minutes to get here. Ramsay would be frozen through if he had to be out in the elements that long."

Starr said, "Unfortunately, it looks to me like we need to handle things here on our own until help can arrive."

"What does that look like?" asked Beatrice. "In terms of handling things, I mean?"

Starr sighed and rubbed her face. "Well, like I mentioned, keeping people safe and warm. Making sure everyone is fed and staying hydrated. Then, I suppose, hanging tight until we can get assistance."

Ivy stood up in a huff. "Clearly our having a relaxing vacation is no longer on the agenda."

Starr said in a tired voice, "Relaxation got preempted."

Ivy stormed out of the lodge. Her flouncing exit was somewhat spoiled when she fell completely flat on her back upon stepping out onto the ice.

Chapter Nine

"Are you all right?" chorused Beatrice, Meadow, and Starr.

"Fine! Absolutely peachy!" spat Ivy. She carefully got up and moved cautiously away after slamming the door shut behind her.

Starr sighed. "I'm afraid everyone is going to be feeling that way soon."

Meadow said, "Maybe she'll have a nice little nap in her cabin and wake up feeling happier."

Meadow, Beatrice reflected, could sometimes be just as optimistic as Wyatt could.

Starr said, "She might. Or she might wake up angrier." She paused. "I do understand why she might be upset. This weekend never should have happened. I put too much faith in the forecasters. Out of an abundance of caution, I should simply have closed the retreat."

"Was that even your decision to make? Or was it the owner's?" asked Beatrice.

Starr considered this and looked a little more upbeat. "Good point. Technically, I do make all the day-to-day decisions for the retreat, but I know the owner's feelings about cancellations. She prefers that the conference center stays open. If we're paying staff, she wants money to be coming in. If I'd consulted her about it, I'm sure she would have said to keep the place open."

"How did the meeting go? How did everyone take the news?" asked Beatrice.

"Well, no one was actually delighted about it, of course. And everyone seemed horrified about Aspen. But what everyone seemed most concerned about was the fact that there was no way to really communicate with anyone outside of the retreat. Everyone pulled out their phones to check, of course, and no one got a signal."

Beatrice said, "Probably we should all put our phones on our chargers to make sure they're fully charged. Just in case."

"In case of what?" asked Meadow. For a creative person, she didn't appear as if she wanted to imagine the worst-case scenario.

"In case we lose power," said Starr grimly.

"There's no backup generator?" asked Beatrice.

Starr shook her head. "Ordinarily, we have no use for it. Honestly, this is the first time I've seen bad weather to this extent."

The door to the lodge opened again. This time there was a sturdy, outdoorsy-looking woman with graying hair, wearing clothes with lots of elastic that looked rather comfy to Beatrice's mind. She wore a pair of bright red rain boots. She waved a hand in greeting, then pulled up a chair next to them in front of the fire.

The woman introduced herself as Cora, then turned to Starr. "You dropped quite a bombshell in there. Everybody is still talking about it."

"Sorry," said Starr. "Was Aspen a friend of yours?"

Cora gave a short, humorless laugh. "No. I'm not sure Aspen really had any friends. She didn't treat people very well."

"What was she like?" asked Beatrice, still trying to get a picture of Aspen.

"Oh, she was one of those people who always seemed to have lots of drama swirling around her. Either she manufactured the drama, or it just happened naturally around her."

Meadow made a face. "That sounds awful. Your guild had a lot to deal with."

Cora nodded. "I don't much care for drama. I liked the way the Sew and Sews were before Aspen joined us. We felt really comfortable with each other. We had a great feeling of camaraderie and were always lending each other a hand. Plus, we just did fun things together. We played games, had swaps, and laughed a lot. It was the kind of guild that liked hanging out with each other even when we weren't quilting. We'd have movie nights or would go out for pizza together. We were also really supportive of each other's art."

"And that changed with Aspen?" asked Beatrice.

"That's right. I mean, at first we were excited about having her join the group. She was young and seemed like a cool person to be around. We figured she might have a lot of ideas and would infuse the guild with new energy." Cora gave that short laugh again.

"And you were disabused of that notion?" asked Beatrice.

"Well, it took a few months. Then we realized Aspen was pulling us all down. She was critical of our quilts, which led to a completely different vibe in the group that hadn't been there before. She also second-guessed *everything*. We had some charitable events that were pretty much set in stone and Aspen would pick those apart. It was like nothing was easy around her. I noticed a lot of the ladies were getting their feelings hurt, too. We have a couple who were insecure about their quilting, and Aspen didn't help."

Beatrice said, "I understood Aspen might have also created issues between the quilters on a more personal level, too."

Cora raised her eyebrows. "Oh, you've heard about Aspen and Ivy's husband, already. Yes, that was pretty disturbing. Especially to Ivy. That stunt had a lot of women in the guild angry with Aspen. Aspen was young, pretty, smart, and talented. She could have easily gotten any single man in town by just crooking her finger. So why go after a married man? And a man married to someone in your quilt guild, at that?"

Meadow nodded, totally absorbed in the soap opera that was unfolding. "Because of the drama. That's what you said, right, Cora? She liked creating drama."

"That she did. She's probably delighted about all the drama she's caused here at the retreat, dead or not," said Cora tartly. "Anyway, it all really upset Ivy, and we tend to protect Ivy. She's sort of delicate. She's one of those people who doesn't react well to stress at all. She has migraines, blood pressure issues, and aches and pains almost like she has the flu."

Beatrice was rather surprised to hear this. Ivy hadn't seemed delicate at all to her. In fact, Ivy had been something of a pill.

Cora continued, "But Aspen's behavior didn't just affect Ivy. It made Olive angry, too. Her brother was married to Aspen and Aspen continued cheating on him." Her voice grew hushed. "He ended up ending his own life."

"Terrible," said Meadow, her eyes sad.

"It was. And Olive kept saying that Aspen was never satisfied with what she had. That she always needed to have more. More people loving her, more money, more drama." Cora shrugged. "Just *more*."

Starr, who'd been sitting quietly and listening, said, "Did you hear any noises last night? See anything?"

Cora shook her head. "No. I slept like the dead last night. I'm ordinarily a pretty light sleeper, and I guess the trip over here tired me out more than I expected. I woke up and discovered a real winter wonderland outside. Couldn't believe it. I almost felt like someone had slipped me a sleeping pill."

Starr said, "I know what you *generally* thought about Aspen. But did you have anything personally against her?"

"Nope. I stayed out of her way as much as possible to keep it that way. Besides, she really didn't have a way to get at me. Aspen probably figured I'd be hard to mess with—I don't really care much what people think."

Meadow looked sad. "I keep thinking how awful it is that your guild was functioning so well until Aspen created all those issues. Do you think things will go back to the way they were before now? In the Sew and Sews?"

Cora considered this. "I'd like to think they could. Like I said, we had such a great group. But Aspen caused so many fractures in so many friendships that it seems almost impossible."

Meadow said, "That makes me sad. Maybe, now that Aspen's gone, you should just double-down and focus on all the ways the Sew and Sews connected before she joined. What brought you all together? Was it an old group or a new one?"

"An old one. Some of our moms actually founded the guild back in the day. Quilting was a family thing for most of us—handed down from older generations. But we also had a lot in common . . . we were friends with some of the same people, had a lot of the same experiences growing up, were from the same town, even if we weren't all the same age. Some of us worked during the week and some of us didn't. We made allowances for everybody's schedule." Cora shrugged, looking wistful. "It was nice when it all started. We weren't trying to make art. We were just enjoying each other's company and quilting."

"And then Aspen joined," said Starr with a quirk of her eyebrows.

"Yes. And she was very good at quilting, to be fair. I suspected that she might have intentionally ramped up her quilting ability before she joined the guild. Just to make sure she *was* the best and could show us all up."

There was a shriek outside and a frantic scrabbling at the door leading into the lodge. The women stood up, looking fearfully at the door. It finally opened with a jerk, revealing Ivy standing there again. Her eyes were huge, and she gasped, "There's a bear out there."

Starr frowned. "Is there?"

Ivy nodded, scrambling away from the door as if the bear might casually open it and join them all by the fire.

Meadow and Beatrice looked at each other. Beatrice said slowly, "The bears should be hibernating now. Or, if it's been too warm for them to do a full-fledged hibernation, they should still be pretty close to their den."

Meadow nodded. "We live in the mountains all year. We've kind of gotten used to their patterns."

Ivy screeched, "I know what I saw!"

Starr cautiously opened the door and peered out. Then she started to chuckle. "Well, I see a couple of deer, looking for food in the snow. Is that what you saw?"

Beatrice wasn't completely sure how Ivy might have mistaken deer for a bear.

Ivy looked cranky. "Okay, I guess I saw them out of the corner of my eye and panicked. But can you see why I *would* have panicked? This whole day has gone completely wrong in every way. No cell service, a huge ice storm, and a dead body. What else could possibly go wrong?"

Meadow winced. "I wouldn't ask that question if I were you."

The door opened again, and the woman Nicole had introduced as her sister, Maggie, walked in. "Is there room for me?" she asked.

Beatrice was glad to see that she didn't seem to be angry anymore about being awakened. If she recognized Beatrice from earlier, she didn't mention it. Instead, she introduced herself to the group. She was wearing a tremendous fur coat and matching fur hat. The extra sleep seemed to have done wonders for her mood.

"Want some coffee?" asked Meadow, nodding to the cup Maggie held.

She shook her head. "Hot chocolate. Coffee makes me too hyper. And hyperactivity isn't exactly great in this closed environment." She glanced over at Starr. "Think you can do something about opening up the fitness center?"

Starr frowned. "The fitness center isn't usually part of the quilting retreat experience."

Maggie snorted. "Being stranded in an ice storm isn't usually part of the quilting retreat experience."

"I'll go open it now," said Starr, looking irritated.

"Oh good!" said Ivy. "I wanted to practice some of my yoga stretches to relieve stress. Do you have yoga mats at the fitness center?"

Starr gave a curt nod and she and Ivy set off.

Maggie took one of the chairs they'd vacated and took a big sip of the hot chocolate. "Glad to see a fire going. I can't seem to get warmed up, even though I have my heaviest winter clothes on."

She did seem to have piled on at least two sweaters and what looked like a couple of pairs of pants. But Beatrice also noticed she still took a great deal of care with her appearance. She was wearing carefully applied makeup and her hair was just so. The coat she was wearing looked like an expensive fur . . . and not a fake one.

"I just can't believe this is happening," said Maggie with a sigh. "This was supposed to be a fun, creative getaway for us all. But the muck of the outside world managed to find us here. It's discouraging."

Meadow nodded sympathetically. "You were at Starr's meeting?"

"Yeah. I thought it was just going to be an advertisement for upcoming retreats for the conference center. I had no idea what she would say. And, judging from the rest of the room, no one else did, either."

But someone had. Someone had known precisely what the meeting would be about and what had happened to Aspen. She shivered.

Meadow said, "Beatrice is going to help find out what happened, since the police can't get here for a while."

Maggie raised her eyebrows and looked Beatrice up and down as if finding it difficult to picture her in some sort of investigator role. "Is that so?"

Meadow nodded and said with pride, "Beatrice has solved lots of cases before the police do. She has a knack for it."

Beatrice flushed and gave a tight smile. If she'd had any thoughts about flying under the radar, Meadow had certainly made that impossible.

Maggie seemed taken aback for a moment before swiftly smiling. "Then you'll want to know what I was doing when poor Aspen perished."

"Do you have an alibi?" asked Meadow, getting into the spirit of the questioning.

This all served to remind Beatrice once again why she disliked having Meadow acting as sidekick.

Maggie drawled, "As it happens, I do. My sister and I were both sleeping the whole night. We'd have woken if the other got up, murdered someone, and came back to bed. The door to our cabin is creaky."

Meadow said, "But you said you slept so soundly!"

Now Maggie gave her an annoyed look. "I did. But there are certain sounds that are bound to wake me up. Like someone stealthily walking out of a cabin. Or my sister getting up in the middle of the night. And vice-versa. Nicole and I are very much the same."

Meadow said wistfully, "I always thought it would be wonderful to have a sister. I didn't grow up with any siblings at all. You and your sister sound like you're very close."

Maggie relaxed a little. "We are. Nicole and I have always gotten along really well. We have a lot in common."

"Who's the older sister?" asked Meadow.

Now Maggie frowned again as if the question were rather insulting. "Nicole, of course."

Meadow quickly said, "Oh, of course." She seemed to realize Maggie thought she'd stuck her foot in her mouth.

"What did you think about Aspen being part of the guild?" asked Beatrice. She was thinking about Cora, and how Cora had blamed Aspen for fracturing the guild.

Maggie shrugged. "I can't worry about things I have no control over. You understand that, surely. And, in some ways, Nicole and I thought Aspen would serve as a breath of fresh air in the group. The guild had fallen into a routine. We didn't try new things anymore. It was comfortable, but it could be stuffy. When Aspen joined, she came with all sorts of ideas for new types of quilts, shows we could attend, and service projects we could work on."

"Aspen was interested in service projects?" asked Beatrice.

Maggie allowed herself a grin. "She wasn't a complete ogre."

"But she *was* difficult to get along with?" asked Beatrice.

"Was she? I don't think Nicole and I really thought so. I mean, Aspen could be a little prickly from time to time, but who isn't? We all have our bad days."

"That's very magnanimous of you," said Beatrice. "Did you have a good relationship with Aspen?"

Maggie gave a little laugh, although there was a flash of displeasure on her face. "I stayed out of her way most of the time. She'd take these little jabs at me from time to time. She'd always tease me about being on my phone too much, for instance. That was just Aspen's idea of a joke. She always had the impression that I was attached to my phone. That I spent way too much time on it." She gave that little laugh again. "Truth be told, I do feel like I'm going through withdrawal right now. I didn't realize just how addicted I am to the thing. It's tough not having any internet or phone connection."

Beatrice thought it was odd that Aspen would call Maggie out on her phone time. She was sure she'd seen Aspen on her phone quite a few times yesterday. Taking selfies of herself, texting, and just looking at it whenever she felt bored. Which seemed to be a lot.

"Who do you think did this, Maggie?" asked Meadow anxiously. "Who killed Aspen?"

Maggie gave her a startled look. "Surely you're not thinking a *quilter* could be behind this?"

Meadow flushed guiltily. Usually Meadow was very reluctant to believe quilters could be involved in skullduggery of any sort. Perhaps she'd started realizing quilters were just like everyone else.

Maggie continued, "Maybe it's this Starr. The director. She knows this place inside and out. She could easily have walked over, murdered Aspen, and then gone back to her house until later on. Nobody knows anything about her, after all."

"Why would she do something like that, though?" asked Beatrice. "She didn't know Aspen."

Maggie shot her an annoyed look. "Well, maybe she did. Maybe she'd known Aspen from another time. She recognized her, understood she posed some sort of risk to her, then eliminated her."

"Wow," said Meadow. She took a few moments to take this in. "And here I was thinking how great she was to walk over in the winter storm to help us out. But she could be the one behind all this."

Beatrice said, "We have absolutely no evidence pointing to the fact that Starr knew Aspen, much less murdered her. It seems a lot more likely that someone in the Sew and Sews guild became upset with Aspen."

"Ivy, for instance," said Meadow, nodding. "That sounded like a mess."

Maggie made a face. "Yes, that was a problem in the group, for sure. Aspen could have had a relationship with pretty much any man she wanted to. It wasn't very sporting of her to choose to have one with poor Ivy's husband. I don't even think she was all that interested in him—it was just the thrill of the chase that made her do it. She seemed to be bored with him almost immediately and started looking around for her next conquest."

There was a crack of thunder outside and Meadow squealed. "What was that?" she cried. "Gunshots?"

"Thunder," said Beatrice grimly. "I suspect we're getting thunder snow."

Maggie sighed. "The forecast was totally botched. I hate it when the forecasters seem so sure and then they're *completely* wrong." She pulled her cell phone out again and glared at the device. "I'm going to try again."

"Remember, the more you use it, the more you're wearing the battery down. You need to put it on the charger after this," said Beatrice.

Meadow was already punching in the phone number. Her eyes grew big. "It's ringing! It's ringing!"

Chapter Ten

The other women stared at her.

"Ramsay? Oh, Ramsay, it's me. No, we're fine. Yes, Beatrice and the rest of our quilters are all safe so spread the news." Meadow frowned. "Ramsay? Ramsay?" She lowered the phone. "We got disconnected."

"Did he hear the part where you said we were all safe?" asked Beatrice intently.

"We're not *all* safe," said Maggie, sounding annoyed.

Meadow ignored her. "Yes, I'm sure he heard that. The phone made a clicking sound right after I said we were safe. He'll spread the word about that, I know." She tried phoning again, this time with no luck. "So frustrating, though. I didn't even have a chance to tell him about the murder here."

"Maybe that's just as well," said Beatrice. "They're ninety minutes away from here and it would be dangerous for Ramsay or anyone else to attempt to reach us on those roads. Besides, the local police have been informed. I'm sure they'll get here as soon as they're safely able to do so."

Maggie tried her own phone again before putting it back down with a sour expression. "Nothing."

Beatrice said, "I'm going to practice what I preach and put my phone on the charger in the cabin."

Meadow stood up. "I'll do the same."

Maggie grunted. "Mine's still fine. Plus, it's freezing in that cabin. Clearly those windows don't provide any insulation whatsoever. I'll stay here by the fire."

On the way to the cabin, Meadow and Beatrice passed the dining hall. They saw Savannah and Georgia stepping out cautiously onto the wintry mix covering the ground. The women spotted them and raised their hands in greeting. Unfortunately, the gesture nearly toppled Savannah, who was often rather awkward. Georgia grabbed hold of her sister to steady her and almost fell down, too.

"Be careful!" called out Meadow.

"Are you heading back to the cabin?" asked Georgia.

"We've got to charge our phones," said Beatrice.

Georgia said, "Good idea. We'll do the same. Then, do you want to join up? I want to talk over what's going on. But I kind of want to do it in private, you know?"

Beatrice said, "Why don't you come over to Piper's and my cabin? It's cabin two. We have a decent-sized sitting area in between our two rooms."

And so, just five minutes later, the women were all sitting in cabin two. Piper was there, as well, and pulled up another chair from inside her bedroom to join them. Beatrice pulled out extra blankets from the closets and handed them out to everyone. She then peered at the tiny kitchenette. "Anyone want hot tea?"

Everyone did. Piper helped Beatrice warm up cups of water and put tea bags in them. Then they settled into the sitting area where the women were quietly chatting.

Georgia gave them a wan smile. "Thanks. Wow, I almost feel like we're really having a retreat right now. Everything else has overwhelmed that fact. I'm so glad we're all here together."

"Me too," said Piper.

Beatrice asked, "Did you all make it over to the dining hall for Starr's meeting?"

Georgia and Savannah nodded.

Piper said, "Even though I overslept, I was able to make it over there. I woke up when I heard Starr's announcement over the intercom." She looked at Beatrice. "When I woke up, you weren't around."

Beatrice winced. "I'm sorry. I sneaked out this morning because I didn't want to wake you up. I figured since you were always being awakened in the middle of the night with a baby, it would be good to have at least one morning where you could actually sleep in."

"Thanks," said Piper wanly. "But why do I have the feeling you had an adventure while I was asleep?"

Savannah frowned ferociously. "Beatrice, you weren't the one who discovered that body, were you?"

Beatrice sighed. "I promise that I had no idea I was doing anything even remotely dangerous. It was the first night in a new location, which means I usually don't sleep very well. Like I said, I was trying to be quiet and just slip out for a while until I became sleepy again. I thought I might do a little quilting or read my book for a few minutes. The ground was already something of a mess, so I picked my way across it carefully to the conference center. Just thinking I'd kill some time."

"And instead you found a body," said Piper.

Beatrice nodded. "Pretty much right off the bat. Of course, I recognized Aspen." She glanced around the group of women. "Did any of you make any observations about Aspen? Or about how she interacted with any of the other Sew and Sews?"

Piper, who still looked disgruntled that her mother had been traipsing around finding bodies, shook her head. "I don't think I noticed anything that you didn't, Mama. I was with you most of the time. I realized Aspen's other guild members did look tense when she was around. And Aspen seemed like she picked at them."

Savannah looked grim. "I sat in the lodge for a while last night and played a chess game on my phone. I was off in a chair on the side of the room, but I could still hear all sorts of things."

"Like what?" asked Meadow, eyes wide.

Savannah pressed her lips together into a thin line. "Squabbling. They were all fussing at each other, plain and simple."

Meadow pressed some more. "But what *type* of squabbling? Who was fussing at who?"

Savannah considered this. "Well, of course, I was playing my chess game. I do tend to get pretty absorbed when I do. One must really pay attention if one is going to beat a computer."

Beatrice hid a smile. Savannah was the type of person who got absorbed in *any* activity she was doing. She was the perfect candidate to play chess on her phone. The structure of the game, the many rules and limited moves, would appeal to an order-loving person like Savannah.

"I suppose the impression I got," said Savannah slowly, "was that Aspen was causing mischief."

Beatrice now smiled broadly. "That's exactly the word one of the Sew and Sews used to describe Aspen's activities. Mischief."

Savannah looked pleased at this, puffing up a bit. "Was it? Yes. That's precisely what Aspen was doing. She was pushing people's buttons. Making snide comments and waiting for the reactions. I got the impression she was really enjoying the reactions she was causing."

Georgia frowned. "I didn't spend much time around her at all. I'm getting the feeling she wasn't a nice person, though."

"That's what I'm gathering," said Beatrice. "Of course, it doesn't mean that she deserved what happened to her. But it could explain *why* it happened. Why someone got upset enough with Aspen to . . . do what they did."

Piper sighed. "I'm so sorry you had to see that, Mama. What an awful shock. You were just there to do some quilting and relax."

"It's okay. It might have been better that I saw it than someone who was close to Aspen. Although Olive did come by soon after I found Aspen."

Georgia asked, "How are the Sew and Sews taking it?"

"They've been very solemn over her death, of course. No one is celebrating, naturally. But it also seems that no one is particularly heartbroken about Aspen. They all tend to think she reaped what she sowed."

Savannah muttered. "She was definitely *sowing* last night. I wish now that I'd paid more attention to what was being said. I just got general impressions, and I don't even know the names of the women. Plus, like I mentioned, I was absorbed in my game."

Meadow asked, "Could you *describe* some of the quilters who were there?"

Savannah's brow crinkled in concentration. "Well, there was a middle-aged woman there. Pretty. But she looked exhausted."

"That sounds like Ivy," said Beatrice. "Could you hear what Aspen was saying to her?"

"It was mostly what Ivy was saying to *Aspen*," said Savannah. "She was basically telling her off for being a terrible person. I didn't really pay attention to why she thought that." She frowned again, trying to remember. "There was also a woman there who made me feel sort of underdressed. She was wearing a fur coat, and I don't think it was fake fur." Savannah, an animal lover, looked even more displeased than she already did.

Beatrice nodded. "That's probably Maggie."

"She was being very sharp with Aspen. But that's probably because Aspen kept carping at her about something." Savannah shrugged. "I didn't pay too much attention why, because it didn't seem important at the time. It just seemed like they were all picking at each other. It made me glad to be a Village Quilter."

Meadow said, "Exactly. That's exactly right. We never carry on like that in our group."

"But we don't have an Aspen in our group," said Georgia slowly. "Somebody who seemed to like a lot of drama."

"Speaking of people in our group, where's Posy?" asked Beatrice. "Has anyone seen her this morning?" She felt a rising worry that something could have happened to the sweet quilter.

Meadow raised her hand as if she were in school. "I have. She ate breakfast, then felt chilly and decided to put on heavier clothes. I'm sure we'll see her again soon."

Beatrice said, "Oh, we forgot to tell them something important, Meadow. That you were able to get through to Ramsay."

The other women perked up at this. Georgia said, "Did you? What did he say? Is help coming?"

Meadow looked sad. "It wasn't that long of a conversation. But what Beatrice is referring to is that I told him to let everybody know we were all okay. I know he heard that part. But I wasn't able to tell him what had happened here or anything. I guess we'll just have to wait until the roads are safe enough for the police to get over here."

Georgia smiled. "I feel so relieved, though. I hated the thought of Tony worrying about me and not being able to get in touch with me."

Meadow said, "I'm worried about *worrying*. I feel like now that quilting has mostly been taken off the table, we're all going to sit around, twiddle our thumbs, and be anxious about getting rescued. We should brainstorm what we can do today."

The women walked back to the lodge, chatting about ideas for things to do. When they arrived in the lodge, Savannah brightened.

"Games," said Savannah simply. "That's what we should do. There's a stack of them on the shelves." She pointed to a shelving unit in the corner of the room where, sure enough, there were plenty of board games and packs of cards.

"Good going," said Meadow. "That's a start."

Georgia said with a crooked smile, "I guess we could raid the cookie sheets from the kitchen and go sledding. That ice out there will make it really slick."

Meadow made a face. "Unfortunately, that's only a good suggestion for the younger quilters in the group. One of which I am decidedly *not*." She mulled on the issue for a moment. "All walks have been taken off the table, too, which is a pity. I've gotten addicted to my daily walk."

"Considering we could barely make it from point A to point B out there, I think walking for exercise is totally impossible," said Beatrice wryly. "But Maggie did get Starr to open up the fitness center for her and Ivy. Maybe we can go check it out later and come up with our own exercise routines."

Savannah said, "Mm. Or we could play games."

Beatrice smiled at her. "Or we could play games."

Meadow said, "Remember, we wanted to establish relationships with the Sew and Sews. We could see if any of them want to join us in a game."

No one looked quite as enthusiastic as Meadow did.

"Isn't one of them a killer?" asked Georgia in a small voice. "They all seem really nice, but somebody killed Aspen. And it sure wasn't a Village Quilter. There's no reason Starr would do it, either."

Beatrice said, "True. I don't think the problem extends to playing games with them, though. I'd say that we probably need to travel in groups, however, and make sure everyone knows where we are." She paused. "With that in mind, I'm going to check in on Posy and make sure she's doing all right."

Meadow leaped up to join her. "We'll track her down, Beatrice."

"Let's try her cabin first."

On the way to Posy's cabin, they saw Olive walking back in the direction of the lodge. Meadow bubbled out a greeting, but Olive seemed to look right through her.

"Did she just totally ignoring me?" asked Meadow, frowning.

"I think she was distracted. We all have a lot on our minds."

To their relief, Posy answered her knock on the door right away. "Hi there, you two," she said with a smile. "Come inside! It's freezing out there." Posy shivered. "Or below freezing."

Meadow gave her a tight hug. "Glad to see you're fine. I'm going to head back to the lodge and play a game with the others. We'll visit later, okay?" And Meadow bounded off.

Beatrice watched until Meadow got safely back to the lodge. Then she stepped into the cabin. "We were just coming by to check on you and make sure everything was okay. Nobody had laid eyes on you for a little while. Ordinarily, that wouldn't be a big deal, but with everything going on right now with the storm, and with Aspen, of course, I wanted to see you."

Posy said, "I'm sorry! That hadn't even crossed my mind. Should we all be staying in groups?"

"That's what we were talking about earlier. We think that might be safer for lots of reasons."

Posy nodded solemnly. "I understand you were the one to find Aspen. What a horrible thing. She was such a pretty girl."

Trust Posy to find something positive to say about Aspen. "She was, yes. I'm sure there's no reason for alarm, but we thought sticking in groups was probably for the best."

"I'll go back to the lodge with you, then, if that's where everybody is."

Posy proceeded to bundle herself up with a huge coat that she seemed to disappear into, a fluffy hat that looked handmade, and a pair of thick gloves. Thus prepared, they stepped outside.

Beatrice noticed that the weather had worsened in the few minutes she was inside speaking with Posy. There was more ice coming down, and gales of wind blew it right into their faces.

"Mercy!" said Posy. "I feel like I should have a ski mask on."

Beatrice nodded grimly. She didn't want to worry Posy, but she had the terrible feeling that the electrical grid wasn't going to be able to handle much more ice. She was surprised they hadn't lost power already.

The two women hurried into the lodge. Posy gave a relieved sigh at the relative warmth of the room, hastily taking off the heavy coat.

The others were playing a board game and looked up as the door opened.

There was a chorus of greetings for Posy.

Posy blushed a little. "Sorry to worry everybody. I was just dithering around in the cabin."

"Why don't you two join us for a game?" said Georgia. "We could use more players."

Beatrice demurred. "If it's all right, I'll just cheer you all on."

Meadow nodded and said to the others, "Beatrice is going to help us figure out who's at the bottom of all this. Especially since the police can't get over here."

Beatrice wasn't sure if Meadow's outsized confidence in her sleuthing abilities made her feel confident or insecure. She decided a change of subject was in order. "What are you playing?" asked Beatrice.

"Monopoly," said Savannah, her gaze eagerly returning to the board game. "I'm the banker."

"As you should be," said Beatrice, "considering you're a CPA."

"I've just dispersed the money to everyone and put the chance cards and the community chest cards out. So we're about to start."

Olive opened the door to the lodge and peered inside as if looking for someone.

"Come play with us!" said Meadow in a jolly voice.

Olive frowned. "I'm not sure it's entirely appropriate to be playing children's games when someone has just lost her life."

Meadow's face fell. "I'm sorry."

"We didn't mean any disrespect," said Piper quickly. "We were just trying to pass the time and keep our minds off the tragedy."

Meadow nodded in agreement. "It's such a terrible thing. We're just trying to make the best of a bad situation."

Olive shrugged a little as if she'd already forgotten what they'd been talking about.

"Were you looking for someone in particular?" asked Beatrice.

Olive looked at her sharply. "What makes you think that?"

Beatrice lifted an eyebrow. "It appeared you were searching for someone when you looked inside the lodge."

Olive shook her head impatiently. "I just have a headache. I'm not myself."

"Maybe you should get a little caffeine," suggested Meadow. "I always have a headache when I don't have the right amount of caffeine."

Olive said wryly, "I won't sleep at all tonight if I have any caffeine after eleven in the morning."

"Really?" asked Savannah, staring at her. Savannah was something of an addict when it came to caffeine. Beatrice remembered she'd been drinking Diet Cokes constantly before she'd weaned herself off on coffee and cut back a bit. The effect of caffeine on Savannah had served to make her more agitated and nervous—which didn't work well with Savannah's personality.

"What about trying decaf?" suggested Posy. "It will still have a tiny bit of caffeine in it and might help your headache."

Olive paused. "Actually, that might help. Thanks."

Meadow said, "I noticed the lodge has a little coffee station out this door and down the hall. It's a small room right before the restrooms."

Olive set out to make her decaf and the rest of the group started the game. It was very much a starting and stopping process because Sew and Sews kept entering the lodge and being enthusiastically encouraged to play by Meadow. By the end, there were eight women playing Monopoly. Beatrice hadn't even realized that many players could do so. Even more quilters had come in and out—visiting, but not playing, before heading back out the door of the lodge. Miss Sissy had joined the game and seemed to have a tremendous amount of money. Beatrice was about to be extremely impressed until she saw the old woman surreptitiously stealing from the bank.

Beatrice moved her chair away from the fireplace and along the side of the room so that she could read and not be in the maelstrom of the game. And it was indeed a maelstrom—Meadow was playing entirely too energetically and endangering the various houses and hotels on the gameboard. The other women were getting caught up in the game too and it had become quite lively with wealthy landowners and players who kept finding themselves in Monopoly jail. Miss Sissy broke all the rules by refusing to go to jail and continuing to rob the bank.

However, it was also a bit too lively for Beatrice to be able to pay attention to her book. She went back to her cabin to get headphones and her phone charger. She figured she could listen to music on her phone as long as the device was plugged in. She put on some soothing jazz music, put her earbuds in, and picked back up with the story. Lucy, the golden retriever, came over for a snuggle, and Beatrice made room next to her on the padded bench she was sitting on. Patting Lucy was soothing and helped Beatrice let go of some of the stress she'd been feeling. And Lucy enjoyed it too, grinning up at her with her eyes half-closed.

At one point, Olive headed for the door. She gave Beatrice a small wave.

"Headache still bad?" asked Beatrice sympathetically after she pulled her earbuds out. She supposed, at least, that Olive's scowl was due to the headache. She certainly looked unhappy.

Olive said, "I'm going to lie down for a while. The decaf didn't seem to help much."

She left and Beatrice continued with her book and with petting Lucy. The Monopoly game went on and on, as Monopoly games do. Beatrice ended up finishing the novel, and the game was still in progress.

Meadow apparently decided that everyone needed to take a break. "How about if we pause for a few moments and everyone share something about themselves or their family?"

Beatrice had the feeling that she knew where this was heading.

"It'll be like show-and-tell," said Meadow with a smile. "I'll start."

Beatrice raised an eyebrow, waiting for Meadow to pull her phone out. She had a feeling she knew the subject of Meadow's show-and-tell.

Meadow continued, "I wanted to share that I love our quilting guild. And I *especially* love it when I can bring my grandbaby along. He livens everything up."

Piper said in a rueful voice, "That's one way of putting it. He can also be a little distracting."

"In the very best of ways," insisted Meadow. "He charms everybody. Even Miss Sissy can't get enough of him."

Miss Sissy glared at Meadow, clearly remembering that Meadow didn't let the old woman have as much one-on-one time with Will as she'd prefer.

"Since he can't be here in person, I've got a few pictures and videos on my phone to share," said Meadow.

Beatrice groaned, and she and Piper shared a look. Beatrice called from the side of the room, "Meadow, no one is going to be as interested in our grandchild as you and I are. As charming and beautiful as he is."

"He's perfect," said Meadow complacently. "And it will only take a few minutes."

As Meadow regaled the group with cute pictures and videos of Will imperfectly singing the alphabet song, Beatrice said to Piper, "Did you bring any extra books with you? I've just finished the one I brought. It probably wasn't the best choice for this trip, considering it was a murder mystery." Beatrice made a face.

"No, I think that's probably not the best pick for right now. I did bring extra books because I knew I was going to finish the one I'd brought with me. And I just did, before falling asleep last night."

"Perfect. What's the name of it?" asked Beatrice.

"*The Thirteenth Tale*. Have you read it?"

Beatrice shook her head. "It doesn't involve murder, does it?"

"It's spooky, but no murders. It's more of a gothic story. It does feature a fire."

Beatrice said, "I'll borrow it from you, if that's okay. I was thinking it might be good for me to try to wind down a little with a book in between talking with everyone about what happened last night."

"Good idea," said Piper. "This is a really stressful situation."

"For everybody."

"Yes, but especially for you." She lowered her voice, although there was no way anyone could hear her over the sound of Meadow, loudly singing Will's praises. "You're the one who's basically having to quiz a bunch of strangers on whether they murdered a friend of theirs."

Beatrice looked grim. "That *is* stressful, when you put it that way."

"I just want to make sure you take care of yourself, that's all."

Beatrice gave her a quick smile. "I'll be fine."

"Want me to go grab the book for you?" asked Piper.

"No thanks. I'd like to get a little fresh air. It's starting to feel a bit stuffy in here." She gave the golden retriever one last rub and stood up, stretching as she did.

A few moments later, Beatrice set foot carefully outside. The ice had accumulated, making walking very tricky. She felt her feet slide out from under her more than once, but was able to stay upright.

She nearly toppled over, however, when she heard a shriek from inside one of the cabins.

Chapter Eleven

Moving as quickly as she could, she rushed in the direction of the scream. When she got outside the cabin, she saw Cora bolt out, her face white and her eyes huge.

"What's wrong?" asked Beatrice tersely.

Starr apparently heard the scream too and came rapidly out of the dining hall. "What's going on?" she demanded.

Cora's mouth trembled. "It's Olive. She's dead."

Starr and Beatrice hurried into the cabin as Cora sank down on the porch of the small building as if not trusting her legs to hold her up.

"Let's not touch anything but Olive," said Beatrice quietly. "Just in case."

Olive was in the bed, eyes open and staring sightlessly into space. A pillow lay partially on her chest.

"Oh no," grated Starr.

Beatrice felt for a pulse, but knew it was futile. Olive was clearly gone.

"What happened?" asked Starr quietly. "She was just fine earlier. You saw her, too."

Beatrice said, "Let's leave the cabin. Can you lock it up behind you?"

"But her roommate won't be able to get in."

Beatrice shook her head. "Her roommate was Aspen, remember? We should block off the area to preserve it for the cops whenever they get here."

Starr muttered, "If they *can* get here. The weather has gotten even worse."

As they were moving away, Beatrice glanced around them. Everything seemed to be in order. But she wondered about the pillow that had been lying partially on top of Olive's chest. Had someone smothered Olive?"

Once outside, Cora looked at them fearfully. "Could you wake her up?"

Beatrice shook her head. "She was gone."

Cora gave a sob, then seemed to try to pull herself together.

There was yelling again, this time coming from the dining hall.

Starr hissed, "What's going on?"

Maggie stepped out of the building and, spotting Starr, glared at her. "Now the power is out! What are we supposed to do with no power?"

It was just as Beatrice had feared. It didn't take much ice to bring power lines down and they'd certainly had a lot of it.

Starr waved her hand at her. "I've got other problems right now." She turned and, fishing in her pocket, pulled out a set of keys. She carefully locked the cabin door behind her and looked at Beatrice. In a low voice she said, "We've got to figure out what's going on. Who knows how long it will take the police to get here?"

Beatrice nodded. "Should we talk with the Sew and Sews individually?" She glanced over at Cora, but the woman was still staring blankly out into the storm. "An office, maybe? Perhaps one with plenty of natural light, since we don't have power now, apparently?"

Starr nodded. "My office. There are windows there and no one can listen in." She paused. "I understand you have some experience doing this. However, I'm in charge of the conference center. I'll allow you to take the lead on asking questions, but I must be involved in the process as a representative of the retreat."

Considering Starr at first was even reluctant to allow Meadow to cook food for the group, it seemed like quite a concession. Beatrice nodded.

Starr muttered, "We should probably speak to Cora first."

Cora, hearing her name, momentarily jerked back into reality. "What are we doing?"

"We're going to chat with you in my office for a minute," said Starr. "We need to gather all the information we can about what happened."

"I don't want to chat with you. I don't want to chat with *anybody*," said Cora. "I just want to go back to my cabin and lock the door. I want to get away from everybody."

Beatrice said, "We know it's hard. But we must figure out what's going on. As soon as we're done speaking with you, you can go to your cabin." A frigid blast of air hit them and she added, "Plus, we want to get inside."

Reluctantly, Cora followed Starr and Beatrice to Starr's office. But first, they had to make their way through the lodge. There, the quilters had picked back up with playing Monopoly, and the game had become even more raucous in the interim. As they came in, Meadow asked cheerfully, "Come to cheer us on? Nicole has Boardwalk, but Savannah has hotels on all the green properties. It's a nail-biter."

She quickly grew solemn when she realized how grim the women looked. "Mercy, what's happened?" asked Meadow.

Starr paused. Then she said slowly, "I'd like to announce what happened during another group meeting, but the dining hall doesn't have enough light. I'm afraid there's been another death." There was an explosion of cries, and she hurried on, "It was Olive. I'm so sorry."

Ivy, who'd been watching the game, croaked, "What? Are you sure? She was just here."

Starr nodded. "We're sure." She held up her hand as Ivy and the other Sew and Sews started asking questions at once. "We just don't have a lot more information than that. I want to let you know that we're trying to get to the bottom of this. Beatrice has helped her local police department with cases previously. And I will be assisting her in her inquiries."

Maggie said angrily, "How do we know Beatrice wasn't involved?"

Meadow glared at her. "Beatrice didn't even know these women!"

Maggie shrugged. "But for all we know, she could be some sort of homicidal maniac."

The women all stared at Beatrice in her puffy jacket as if she might pull a hatchet out of her pocket at any moment.

"Ridiculous!" said Savannah severely. "Beatrice is the sanest person I know."

The other Village Quilters murmured their assent. Piper said, "As her daughter, I can attest to that."

"Then what about Starr?" said Maggie in a huffy voice. "She could be involved. How can we trust her?"

Starr said coldly, "I've never met Aspen in my life. Why on earth would I want to kill her?" She waved her hand again, more dismissively this time. "This is using up valuable time. As I stated, we're going to start speaking with everyone now. We've got to gather information that could help keep us all safe."

Beatrice nodded. "We'll be speaking with the Village Quilters, too. Although none of us knew Aspen or Olive, we might have important information that can serve as clues to help us figure out what's happened."

Starr motioned Beatrice and Cora to follow her and they left the room, where the women's voices were raised as they tried to absorb what was happening.

Starr's office was in the back of the lodge, tucked away from busier areas. It was a plain, tidy room and, as promised, had plenty of natural light. But Starr was already thinking ahead to later in the day when the light would be waning. "Best to pull these out now," she muttered as she grabbed a couple of battery-powered lanterns from a storage closet. She sighed. "I'm afraid it's going to start getting cold in here soon, with the power out. But I don't think we can commandeer the area in front of the fireplace. I'll get some blankets in here later."

Cora took a seat in front of Starr's desk and Starr motioned Beatrice to sit behind her desk and shoved a notebook and a pen her way.

Cora looked wearily at the two women. "What is it you want to know?"

Beatrice gave her a sympathetic look. "I know this is tough. If you're able to, I think it would be very helpful if we hear how you came to find Olive. Can you walk us through that? Were you looking for her for some reason?"

Cora nodded. Although she'd been rather gregarious the first time Beatrice had spoken with her, she now seemed almost removed, as if she had a filter in place as emotional protection. "I wanted to borrow a pair of earbuds from her. She'd mentioned earlier that she had an extra pair. I'd thought I could relax for a little while and listen to some podcasts."

Starr raised her eyebrows. "Podcasts? With no wi-fi?"

"I'd downloaded them before I left home," said Cora in a listless voice. "No wi-fi needed."

Beatrice gave her a friendly smile. "That was smart. I wish I'd put a little more time into planning this trip."

Cora gave a small smile in return. "I always like to have stuff downloaded for a road trip. You never know when you're going to hit a pocket where you don't have any reception. Anyway, I knocked on Olive's door to get the earbuds. She didn't answer. I thought that was weird because I'd just told her I was going to be coming by."

Beatrice said, "When I'd seen Olive earlier, she wasn't feeling very well. Maybe she'd decided to put her feet up for a few minutes."

Starr's eyes narrowed. "You think Olive might have had a natural death?"

"No," said Beatrice. "But it's interesting. Did she say anything to you about it, Cora?"

"She didn't. Although she kept rubbing her temple as if her head hurt," said Cora slowly. "It didn't occur to me that she might have gone to lie down or anything, though. I thought maybe she was in the restroom, so I just waited for a while outside the cabin. Until I started getting really cold."

"Which probably didn't take long," said Beatrice.

"Exactly. So I started knocking a little louder. Then I just decided to walk in." She gave another small shrug. "You know the rest."

Beatrice said, "Right. Unfortunately, I think it's going to be helpful to know everyone's movements prior to finding Olive. Could you help fill me in?"

Beatrice held her breath. She thought Cora might raise an objection to this, but instead she looked disinterested.

"Sure. It's not all that interesting. I was in the dining hall for a while, having a snack and getting a hot drink. I tried to make a phone call without any luck. Olive was in there, and I mentioned the earbuds to her. She told me she had an extra pair that she could lend me."

"But you didn't immediately follow her there to get them?" asked Starr with a frown.

"No. Olive wanted to talk with somebody."

Beatrice and Starr looked at each other. "Do you know who Olive wanted to speak with?"

"No. I didn't ask. She seemed really preoccupied to me, so I just told her I'd grab them from her later. Then I walked back to the lodge and watched the Monopoly game. Later, I was ready to find something to do, so I went back out to find Olive."

Starr said, "I guess the women playing the Monopoly game couldn't have done it."

Cora snorted. "Of course they could have. Everyone was getting up all the time. They'd get up to get coffee or to use the bathroom or head to the dining hall to get a quick snack. Everybody had opportunity."

Beatrice said, "How well did you know Olive?"

"I knew her well. We all did. Olive was an integral member of the guild." Cora stopped and seemed to swallow hard. After a moment, she said, "Unlike Aspen, she's sure to be missed."

Starr said, "You weren't fond of Aspen."

"*No one* was fond of Aspen. I firmly believe Aspen preferred it that way. The only thing any of us liked about Aspen was her quilting skills. It's a pity you didn't get the chance to see her at work. She'd have created something amazing this weekend. Other than that, yeah. Aspen was a pain. I think it bothered me the most that she seemed so spoiled and entitled. I had to work for everything I had," said Cora.

"You had a tough upbringing?" asked Beatrice.

"It sure was. My dad left my mom when I was just a kid and never supported her. She had two jobs and neither one of them was easy. As soon as I was old enough, I had an after-school job to help pay for my education. Even then, I couldn't pay off my student loans for ages. I thought things would get easier as I got older, but if anything, they've gotten tougher. Mom has memory impairment and lives with me. Everything has been hard." She paused and then said in a bitter voice, "Someone like Aspen wouldn't understand any of that."

"But Olive would have?" asked Starr.

"Olive was great. She didn't come from a rough background like me, but she was very empathetic. This shouldn't have happened. If I'd realized we were in any sort of danger, I'd have made sure everyone stayed together." Her sadness abruptly shifted to anger as she looked at Beatrice. "Who's doing this? If you're such a great sleuth, why can't you figure this out?"

Starr frowned. "I think it's far too early to be leveling criticism, don't you?"

Cora pressed her lips together before saying, "I'm sorry. You're right."

Beatrice asked, "Did you feel like Olive was acting any differently than usual?"

"How do you mean?" Cora frowned.

Beatrice said, "Distracted. Worried. You mentioned that she was preoccupied."

"Well, sure. But aren't we all acting a little differently right now? It's called stress. It makes all of us behave in unusual ways. Maybe Olive was even feeling guilty, you know? Maybe she was relieved Aspen was gone and felt guilty over her reaction."

Starr raised her eyebrows. "But you don't think she felt guilty because she murdered Aspen?"

"No."

Starr pushed more. "If you had to pick someone who might have had something to do with these deaths, who do you think it would be?"

Cora pursed her lips for a moment, thinking.

Beatrice said, "The last time I spoke with you, you seemed to think that Ivy might be responsible."

"Did I?" Cora frowned. "I don't remember saying that."

"You spoke about her motive a little."

Cora said, "Oh, you mean because Aspen was having an affair with her husband. Yeah, that was a thing. But I don't think I said Ivy murdered Aspen. I still find it hard to believe that one of our group did anything at all . . . to Olive, anyway. I suppose Maggie could have killed Aspen. Then, *maybe*, she could have murdered Olive to cover her tracks. I guess maybe Olive knew something—is that the assumption we're operating under?"

Beatrice and Starr nodded. Beatrice asked, "Why do you think Maggie might have been involved?"

"Well, I wasn't going to say anything after Aspen died because I figured it didn't really matter or wasn't pertinent. But now that Olive has died, I think you should know. Maggie has been playing around on her fabulously wealthy husband. Maybe Aspen found out and threatened to let Maggie's husband know about the affair."

Starr's brow creased. "Why would Aspen do that?"

"Because that's the kind of person Aspen was," said Cora. "She liked to stir up trouble."

Beatrice asked, "What would have happened if Maggie's husband found out she was having an affair?"

"He'd have dropped her like a hot potato. Believe me, she'd be living a very different life than the privileged one she's living now."

Starr said, "That must have been very stressful for Maggie. Being worried her secret was going to come out."

"Hey, we're *all* dealing with stress. I'm stressed now, myself. Like I said, my mom has been having all sorts of issues and I've been very worried about her. But most of us don't murder people when we're stressed out. The difference here is that Maggie was worried about Aspen revealing her secret. Maybe she decided to hush her up permanently. Or maybe she didn't. I'm no expert. I'd still like to learn that these murders were perpetrated by some sort of itinerant person who happened into the conference grounds."

Starr looked rather wistful as if she too wished it were that simple.

Then Cora gave a shiver. "If you're all done, I'm ready to get out of this office and warm up by the fire."

Beatrice nodded and Cora quickly took her leave.

Chapter Twelve

Starr said, "Well, it sounds like Maggie is a real possibility. Have you spoken much with her?"

"Yes, but I didn't hear anything about her having an affair. I guess that's to be expected, though. She certainly didn't seem like she was antagonistic toward Aspen at all. I mean, she agreed with everyone else who said Aspen had changed the whole tone for their guild. But she said at first that she and her sister thought Aspen would bring some fresh ideas to the group."

"Sister?" asked Starr, looking distracted.

"That's right. Her name is Nicole."

"Got it," said Starr. "They're rooming together. The different last names threw me."

"Maggie is married," said Beatrice. "Although apparently, she might not be very satisfied with her marriage."

"What else did Maggie talk about?"

Beatrice said, "Well, she mentioned that Aspen often picked at her for being so attached to her phone. It sounded like petty stuff."

Starr nodded. "But if Aspen was threatening to tell Maggie's husband about Maggie's affair, that would be a totally different matter. Not petty at all."

"Yes, but I have to wonder how much of a secret Maggie's affair actually was. If Cora knew about it, maybe other people did, too. Maybe Maggie's husband was the only one who *didn't* know."

Starr said, "Yes, but no one else probably intended on approaching Maggie's husband and filling him in. Aspen was probably the only one who wanted to inflict that kind of damage."

Beatrice said, "And who knows if she was blackmailing Maggie about it? It seems like the kind of thing Aspen might have done, from what I've heard about her." She looked at the battery-powered clock on the wall. "Okay, who's next?"

Starr rubbed her face. "It doesn't even really matter, I guess, as long as we speak to everyone. I have other things I need to tend to."

"Regarding the lack of power ... is the stove gas-powered? Or the oven?"

Starr shook her head grimly. "Not a bit. Everything is electric, which means there's no way to heat up our food. Or cook it." She thought about it. "I guess I could pull out the meat and put it in coolers and stick it outside. It would certainly keep cold that way."

Beatrice said, "The only problem with that is that it might attract animals."

"True. Bears should be hibernating, or at least *somewhat* hibernating. But raccoons might be a problem. We always have them at our bird feeders, and they try to get into our trash sometimes." Starr sighed. "What a mess."

Beatrice said, "I'm not trying to pile on or anything, but don't we need to think about how to keep everybody warm? Especially at night? The cabins are going to be freezing without electricity."

"Oh my gosh. I hadn't even thought about that. I don't know if there's enough room in the lodge for everyone to pull mattresses into the room. And we don't have any sleeping bags."

Beatrice asked, "Do you have many extra blankets? Even though there isn't enough room for everyone to be in front of the fireplace, this building should still be warmer than the cabins, even if people are sleeping in the hallways. We could create pallets. We might not be very comfortable, but we'd be warm."

Starr considered this. "I think in the housekeeping area, there are blankets in storage. I'll check that out." She paused. "Actually, I think I should make a list of all the different things I need to do." She reached over and grabbed herself a notebook and a pen from the desk.

Beatrice said wryly, "Our oldest guild member, Miss Sissy, has been very keen on having s'mores. Maybe a firepit might actually work as a way to cook other food, too."

Starr considered this. "We do have a firepit that's open on the sides but covered on the top. The only problem is that it wouldn't really provide any protection with the weather we're experiencing right now. The way the wind is howling, it's just going to throw ice right into everyone's faces."

"Maybe we should check in with the group as a whole and see if anyone has any ideas. Before we speak to anyone else." Beatrice paused. "There's always the fireplace. We could cook over sticks there."

Starr was already shaking her head. "That would take forever for this group to cook that way."

Beatrice said wryly, "We could always make the s'mores for Miss Sissy. That's one way to keep her from bringing them up again."

"Those would definitely be easy to make. But it might seem a little too festive, given the circumstances."

"Agreed," said Beatrice.

So Beatrice and Starr left the office and headed back to the others. The Monopoly game had been put on hold and everyone seemed listless. They looked up when Beatrice and Starr entered the room.

Starr stood by the fire, facing the women. "Okay. So, we're having some setbacks with the weather. Unfortunately, as you've all noticed, we've lost power. I'm open to suggestions about how we might handle food prep and staying warm so that it works better for us."

Ivy made a face. "How about suggestions about how we can get out of here? There's a *killer* on the loose, in case no one has noticed."

Miss Sissy intoned, "Evillllllll."

The Sew and Sews stared at the old woman. The Village Quilters, on the other hand, didn't even notice the interruption.

Ivy shot Miss Sissy a look and then continued, "We're all in danger, for heaven's sake. It's not safe here. Plus, now we don't even have a way to stay warm or to eat! I say we get out of here while we still can."

Starr was clearly trying to listen patiently to Ivy, but Beatrice could tell she was automatically rejecting her suggestion. She said in a calm voice, "I understand what you're saying. And believe me, there's nothing I'd like more than to get all of us safely out of here."

"No, I don't believe you *do* understand," insisted Ivy. "We're scared. We want to go home. You can even *walk* home, from what I understand."

Beatrice turned to Starr. "She has a point. Do you think your house has power? Or do you have a generator for bad weather?"

Starr shook her head. "Generators cost a lot of money . . . money I don't have. And, like I've said before, this is unusual weather for this area. This will definitely go down in the records as a historical storm. It's highly unlikely that I have power, living as close as I do to the conference center."

Maggie gave Starr a cold look. "Maybe the smart thing would be to go home and see if you do have power. Then you can host us at your house."

Beatrice could tell that Starr didn't want to make the trip. She clearly felt a lot of responsibility for the group and was hesitant to leave anyone alone, especially under the circumstances.

"I can go," suggested Beatrice.

The women all stared at her.

"Mama, no," said Piper, looking appalled. "Didn't you see how slippery it was outside? You'd fall. You might even break something. I can go, instead."

Meadow frowned ferociously. "The mother of my grandson? The weather is awful out there. We can't have anything happen to you. Think how upset Will would be if something terrible happened!"

Starr held up her hands to prevent further talking. "No one else needs to risk it. I'll go. Just to be sure. And maybe I can grab some extra supplies while I'm there."

Beatrice shook her head. "I don't think you should go by yourself."

Nicole said, "I'll go with Starr. I'm feeling kind of stir-crazy in here, anyway. It'll be good to get out and about."

Starr gave her a doubtful look, but finally nodded. "Okay," she said reluctantly. "We'll plan a trip out. But let's do it tomorrow. Today has already been stressful enough. I'm tired, I'm sure Nicole is tired, and it won't be long before we start losing light."

Ivy gave a plaintive cry. "And then it'll be even colder. What are we going to do?"

Posy cleared her throat and everyone turned to look at her. "We probably should all sleep in the same place, shouldn't we? Body heat and that sort of thing?"

Starr said, "That's what Beatrice and I were talking about. Unfortunately, there's not enough space in this room for us to put our mattresses down. But the fire will make it the warmest area."

Miss Sissy made a loud grumbling noise and the Sew and Sews continued to look quizzically at her.

Piper said, "I think mattresses might be tough for us to drag around anyway, especially considering the bad weather outside. Like I mentioned before, the risk is pretty high that someone could fall and get injured. I don't think any of us has any sort of medical background, do we?"

The women looked at each other before shaking their heads.

Piper continued, "Then maybe we should just create some makeshift beds. We can pile up some of the armchair cushions I've seen around the conference. We can take the bedding from our cabins. Then we can lay everything out on the floor. It's not going to be super-comfortable, but we'll be warm."

Beatrice added, "And safe. Something else we should consider is ensuring we're always together. Go everywhere in groups."

The quilters looked solemnly back at her.

Ivy wailed, "Because there's a killer loose. Are we *sure* we can't get away from here?"

Starr shook her head firmly. "There's no way. It would be too easy for a car to go off the side of the mountain."

Ivy gave an unhappy sigh.

Posy cleared her throat and said uncertainly, "I was wondering if perhaps we ought to have a small memorial service for Aspen and Olive."

Piper said, "That's a wonderful idea, Posy."

Thus encouraged, Posy continued, "It's just that I feel bad about them being shut behind locked doors. Out of sight. Of course, I understand why it's important for them to be locked away," she added quickly. "But I think it might be nice if people who knew them said a few words."

The Sew and Sews glanced at each other, looking to see who might volunteer for the task. No one seemed eager to do it.

Posy said, "If it's too tough for the ladies who knew them, I'm sure I could say a few words."

Maggie spoke up then, "No, it makes more sense for someone who knew them to memorialize them. I'm not the best speaker, but I'll do it."

Starr nodded. "Great. And that was an excellent idea, Posy. I was feeling uncomfortable, and I wasn't exactly sure why. Would you like to put that together?"

Ivy drawled, "Surely it doesn't have to be anything formal. After all, we know the location for the service—it has to be in this room. It's the only one with a heat source. None of us likely brought dressy clothes." She looked derisively at Maggie. "Except for Maggie, of course. She dresses up all the time. And it's not like we have food to plan. We don't even have a way of cooking food."

Posy looked slightly deflated and Beatrice quickly spoke up, "No, it won't be formal. But it might be nice to allow Maggie a bit of time to figure out what she wants to say. And maybe to arrange the room so that everyone can see Maggie when she eulogizes the women."

Posy smiled at Beatrice.

Maggie said, "I won't need much time. Maybe we should do it right after dinner." She paused. "Speaking of dinner, do we have any sort of plan for that? Is the food spoiling in the fridge and freezer as we speak?"

"It's not spoiling yet because we haven't opened the doors since the power went off. But I'm planning on putting the food in coolers outside to keep it fresh. As far as cooking it, I suppose we might try grilling outside. There are some covered areas, although the wind might blow snow or ice in through the sides," said Starr.

"S'mores," growled Miss Sissy.

Starr glanced her way.

Beatrice said, "Starr, you've already agreed to head over to your house for supplies. There's no reason you have to do everything. I'm happy to help put things in coolers."

Meadow said, "Nope. Beatrice, your job is to figure out what's going on here. You need to get to the bottom of these murders. I can take care of the food."

Piper said, "Why don't you focus on cooking, Meadow? I'll help load the food into coolers and put it outside."

"Georgia and I will help you," said Savannah.

That having been decided, Beatrice said, "We're going to be speaking with everyone, as we've mentioned before. One of us may have witnessed something helpful and may not even be aware of it. I appreciate everyone's cooperation."

Nicole stood up. "I'll speak with you now."

Starr looked at Beatrice, "I'm going to let you handle this. I think I should take a look at the fuse box and make sure it's genuinely a power outage and not some tripped circuit breakers. Plus, I'll grab those extra blankets from storage."

Nicole followed Beatrice into Starr's office. Sher gave a shiver. "I'm glad Starr's going to hunt down those blankets. It feels pretty arctic in here."

Beatrice sat down behind Starr's desk again and flipped to a new page of the notebook as Nicole plopped down into the chair in front of the desk. Beatrice noticed that Nicole seemed more agitated, more fidgety, than she had when she'd spoken to her before. But then, there was more reason to be agitated.

Nicole said, "Do you think you'll really be able to figure out who's doing this?"

Beatrice gave a little shrug. "I'm not sure, but I feel I've got to try. We'll feel a lot safer if we know what happened to Aspen and Olive. And why it happened."

Nicole rubbed her face. "That's what I don't get. I don't understand why somebody would kill Olive." She gave a short laugh. "I *totally* get why someone would have wanted to kill Aspen. But not Olive."

"Olive was pretty well-liked in the guild?" asked Beatrice.

"Sure. She was always really involved in our group. She was one of the oldest members of the guild." Nicole suddenly swallowed. "Sorry. I think it's all just starting to hit me. I can't imagine us having meetings and events and not having Olive there."

"So she got along with everyone."

"Yes, generally. I mean, Olive could be kind of prickly, but we all knew that was just her personality. She was always the kind of person to lend a hand with advice—on quilting *or* life. She was a very sensible person. Why someone would *do* this, I just have no idea." Nicole drummed her fingers on her leg, still very agitated. "Aren't you supposed to ask me if I have an alibi or something? Isn't this going to boil down to who had the opportunity to murder Olive?"

Beatrice nodded. "I think you're right. Could you recount your movements?"

Nicole blew out a sigh. "I've been all over the place, so I certainly don't have an alibi. I played Monopoly for a few minutes, but then I ended up quickly going bankrupt. One of the Village Quilters took my place at the table. Then I went to the kitchen to see if I could find a snack. I ended up making hot chocolate instead. After that, I headed back to the cabin for a while to get something for Maggie, who was still playing the game."

"It sounds like you wouldn't be able to give an alibi for anyone else, either. Since you were walking all around the grounds."

Nicole quickly said, "Maggie and I had absolutely no reason to kill Olive." Her chin was squared, and she looked directly at Beatrice.

"What about Aspen?" asked Beatrice.

"You obviously think the two deaths are connected."

Beatrice raised an eyebrow. "It seems pretty certain that they would be. It's hard to imagine that two women would have two completely different people responsible for their deaths, especially in a closed environment like this. It's definitely not an outsider."

"Okay, I get that, but you've already asked me about my feelings about Aspen the last time I spoke with you."

Beatrice said, "I thought you might have more to add, on reflection."

Nicole sat back in her chair, fingers now drumming on the arm.

"Women can be catty sometimes," said Beatrice.

"Cattiness is different from wanting to kill someone. I don't think I have anything else to say about Aspen."

"Can you talk a little more about Olive, then? Any background you can offer on her or how she fit into the group could be helpful. I didn't know her at all, apart from the brief impressions I had of her since we've been here," said Beatrice.

Nicole shot her an impatient look but finally relented. "Olive fit into the group very well. She stepped into leadership roles whenever we needed someone. She ran meetings, planned events, reached out to service organizations we might partner with, and coordinated with other guilds on quilt shows."

It sounded rather like Nicole was building a resume for Olive instead of offering personal information, but Beatrice nodded encouragingly.

Nicole continued, "As far as her personality, she could be very self-contained. A lot of the time, I wasn't completely sure what she was thinking. I mean, we knew Olive wasn't happy about Aspen marrying her brother, but she never said much about it. She just kept that stiff upper lip. She was one of Aspen's bridesmaids and kept a tight smile on the whole time. But I could tell, as time went on, she was less and less happy with Aspen. Even though she didn't say much about it, I could see a muscle in her jaw start working overtime whenever she was around her."

"It sounds like Olive probably wasn't devastated over Aspen's sudden death."

Nicole shook her head. "To be honest, it crossed my mind that Olive might have been responsible for Aspen's murder. Still waters run deep. And Olive was always the protective big sister for her brother. She'd always portrayed her parents as these sorts of hands-off people and said she'd practically raised her brother. I figured she resented Aspen for stepping into that role. Except Aspen couldn't have been farther from a nurturer. She was more of an every-man-for-himself sort of person. She wasn't a caregiver in any way."

Beatrice said, "And Aspen was apparently unfaithful to her husband? From what I've gathered, anyway."

Nicole nodded. "That's right. Completely unrepentant about it, too, as if she didn't totally understand what marriage was supposed to be about. So she didn't only wreck her marriage, she had a hand in wrecking Ivy's, too." She quickly added, "But like I was saying, just because someone was angry at Aspen doesn't mean that they'd kill her."

Nicole moved restlessly in her chair, glancing around the office. Then she froze, squinting at something on the edge of the desk. "What's that?"

"What?" asked Beatrice.

Nicole shoved aside some papers and picked up a book. She studied it for a few moments, then flipped it around and held it out to show it to Beatrice. "That's Aspen."

Chapter Thirteen

Beatrice peered at the book, which seemed to be a yearbook. Sure enough, there was a black-and-white photo of a young woman, smirking back at the photographer.

Nicole narrowed her eyes. "And this is Starr's office?"

"Yes. But what's this doing here? Is this Aspen's yearbook? Did Starr take it?"

Nicole flipped through the book. "No, all the notes in here mention Starr. It's *Starr's* yearbook." She stared at Beatrice. "I thought she said she didn't know Aspen? Maybe *she's* the one who murdered Aspen. If Starr could lie about knowing Aspen, she could lie about anything."

Which was when the door to the office was pushed open and Starr appeared, staring silently at them.

"That's personal," said Starr, striding across the small room and snatching the yearbook out of Nicole's hands.

Nicole stood up, looking combative. "Did you take that from Aspen?"

Starr pressed her lips together and for a second Beatrice wasn't sure if she was going to answer. Then she gave a small sigh. "No. No, it's mine."

Beatrice gave her a sharp look. "So you did know Aspen. Despite what you'd said earlier."

Starr shook her head. "I really didn't. Look, I know this looks bad. But the only reason my high school yearbook is even here is because I grabbed it when I saw Aspen's name on the registration for this weekend. I wanted to refresh my memory as to what she looked like so I could recognize her if she was the same person." She paused. "Her last name was different, so I figured she might be married. I thought it might be her since there aren't that many Aspens running around."

Nicole snorted. "And now there's one fewer."

Starr's face lost color. "I had nothing to do with that. I didn't even know her."

"Really? Because it sure looks like you did," said Nicole.

Starr shook her head. "You're misunderstanding everything. Like I said, I saw the name on the registration lists and brought the old yearbook over here from my house before everyone arrived."

"Because you wanted to finish some old high school business?" asked Nicole with a sneer. "She was a bully in high school and you wanted to get back at her?"

Starr took a deep breath. "Actually, you're not too far off. Except I didn't want to get back at her. I just wanted to take a look at her and maybe feel superior in some way. That's it. And I wasn't lying—I *didn't* know her. Here." She took the yearbook and flipped through it. Then she held it out, pointing to a picture of a girl with thick glasses, braces, and a rash of acne covering her face. "That's me."

Starr flipped back to Aspen's picture. She was blonde and beautiful, confidence streaming from her as she posed for the camera. Starr said, "Now, do you think she would waste her time with someone like me?"

"So you *were* bullied," said Nicole.

Starr shook her head. "She didn't even know who I was. She was one of those girls who was so completely self-absorbed that she didn't pay any attention to anyone else around her. She was a cheerleader, she was in student government, and she was prom queen. Aspen did all the things. I guess part of me, a not-very-nice part, was hoping that she'd show up and *not* be pretty or successful anymore." She gave a short laugh. "Clearly, that was a pipe dream."

Beatrice asked, "Did Aspen recognize you?"

"No! Like I've been telling you, she didn't even know I existed."

Beatrice asked, "Did you tell her who you were? Did you mention to her that you'd been to the same high school?"

Starr shook her head. "I did nothing of the kind. Once I saw she was basically the same person she'd been back in school, I didn't want to spend any time with her at all. Believe me, I had no reason to kill her. It wasn't as if Aspen ruined my life or anything. She was just a girl who thought she was special. Then she clearly turned into a woman who thought the same thing."

Nicole stood up. "Whatever. That's clearly what you'd say even if Aspen *had* bullied you in high school. Now I'm getting out of this office. It's freezing in here." She paused. "I'll still go with you over to your house tomorrow morning. But I'm going to keep an eye on you. I don't totally trust you, Starr."

With that, Nicole strode out of the room.

Starr plopped down into the chair she'd vacated, looking at Beatrice across the desk. "You believe me, don't you?"

Beatrice wasn't completely sure she did. "Why didn't you say something earlier? About having known Aspen?"

Starr rubbed her temples. "Because I *didn't* know her. And because of this very same reason—I knew that it was going to get blown out of proportion. I knew I hadn't laid a finger on Aspen, and it was just going to distract from the investigation if I was considered a suspect." She got up and shut the office door before glancing out in the hall to make sure no one was around. "I wanted to tell you something. I'd overheard Maggie and Nicole earlier, talking with each other. It wasn't long before Cora found Olive."

"You could hear what they were saying?" asked Beatrice.

"Not well, but enough. They were trying to be quiet, but their voices kept getting louder. It sounded like Aspen had been blackmailing Maggie."

"Did it? Did you hear any details?"

"I didn't get a chance to hear more. But that's pretty significant. If Maggie was being blackmailed, it shows Aspen knew something about Maggie that Maggie didn't want anyone else to know. It doesn't really matter what the secret was. It was clearly something important enough that Maggie would pay Aspen to keep it quiet. So Maggie came into the retreat with a reason to want Aspen dead."

Beatrice said, "That could definitely be the case. Are you saying Nicole is covering up for her sister?"

"Sure. She seemed eager enough to throw me under the bus for not owning up to the fact that I was acquainted with Aspen. It makes sense for her to do that if she were trying to protect her sister."

Beatrice said, "One thing is bothering me. You seem like a smart person. Why didn't you put the yearbook away?"

Starr gave her a rueful look. "Believe me, I'm asking myself the same question. What it boils down to is that I got distracted.

The yearbook and Aspen ended up not seeming important when the storm happened and then when Aspen and Olive were found, so I didn't think anymore about it. Clearly. I should have tucked it away before I offered my office to you. Or maybe, subconsciously, I wanted to get caught. It could be that I felt guilty about hiding the fact Aspen and I had gone to school together."

"Okay. I'm sure word is getting out now that you knew Aspen. If you're wanting to get ahead of that, maybe you should address the group again."

"Right. I've also got to get on with figuring out what we're going to eat and how to help Meadow with food prep." Starr absently pushed a lock of hair out of her eyes. "I guess I should get on that. It's going to get dark soon, and that's not going to help anything."

Beatrice said, "Do you have enough wood for the fire? I know no one was planning to be burning it all day and all night."

"Well, we'll definitely run out after a while, but I'm sure the authorities will get here before then. It's dry, but it does have to be removed from a storage shed on the property and hauled over to the lodge. I'll take care of that after looking into the food prep."

Beatrice shook her head. "You're taking on too much. What we should be doing is coming up with a rotation for these things. You're still looking at the situation from the perspective of a staff member running a retreat. You're not taking into account the emergency aspect of it all."

Starr said wryly, "That's probably because the guests aren't taking the emergency aspect into account."

"I haven't heard anyone from the Village Quilters complaining about the lack of amenities."

Starr raised an eyebrow. "Maybe not. But you only have to spend a few minutes with the Sew and Sews before you hear Ivy or Maggie say something. They're apparently not the best sports. But, to be fair, it looks like they've both been coddled for some time."

Beatrice said, "Speaking of Maggie, do you mind asking her to come back here? I think I'll speak with her next."

Starr gave a quick nod and headed out of the office.

The office was becoming chillier by the minute. Beatrice pulled out her gloves and put them on, despite making it harder for her to take notes. A few moments later, Maggie walked in. She was wearing the tremendous fur coat and a matching fur hat. Beatrice supposed she was very warm but agreed with Savannah that the pieces were likely not faux fur.

Maggie sat down in the chair and gave Beatrice a smirking smile. "Why do I have the feeling I'm in the principal's office?"

Beatrice smiled back at her. "Sorry. That's not the impression I'm trying to give. Starr offered her office, and it seemed like the best place to take notes and not be far from everybody."

"Oh, I heard all about Starr and her office. When I left the group, Starr was still trying to convince everybody that she didn't know Aspen in school." Maggie snorted.

"You don't believe her?"

Maggie said, "No I don't. Don't you remember back to your high school days? I bet you can still remember who you liked and who you couldn't stand from back then."

"Well, it's been a while," said Beatrice with a chuckle. "But I know what you mean. Still, I don't think that sounds like a reason to kill someone you haven't seen for over a decade."

Maggie threw up her hands, which were encased in leather gloves. "We're just taking Starr's word for it that she hasn't seen Aspen since then."

"That's true. But I also think it's telling that Starr retrieved her high school yearbook just to make sure this was the same Aspen."

Maggie's mouth twisted. Beatrice had the feeling she wasn't used to having her opinions challenged and didn't much care for it. She moved on, not wanting Maggie to clam up. For a moment, she wasn't sure how to begin asking questions. Should she start with the biggest one she had? Or should she lead with some easier questions?

While she was considering this, Maggie said, "So I understand we're supposed to play along with you being Sherlock. That you have some experience at this."

Beatrice demurred. "I definitely don't have anything official. It's not as if I worked side by side with the police or anything."

Maggie snorted. "If you listen to Meadow, it sounds like you're single-handedly responsible for keeping the peace in your town."

"No. Actually, Meadow's husband is responsible for that. But with the situation we're in, it was decided it might be good to get a head start on figuring out who's behind this. We want to make sure no one else is affected."

"Killed," said Maggie coolly. "You want to make sure no one else is killed. All right, I'll play. Ask me questions."

Beatrice took a breath, deciding to start with the big question first. "It's my understanding that you did have a good reason for wanting Aspen dead. Despite what you said earlier."

Maggie raised her carefully penciled eyebrows. "Did I? How awful of me. Was it because Aspen said snarky things to me? Because I just don't think that's a good enough reason."

"No. But the fact she was blackmailing you over your affair was."

Maggie's face suddenly lost color, showing her makeup in sharp relief. "What?" she asked in a small voice.

"You were having an affair. Or perhaps you're still having one. I understand you would have a lot to lose if your husband were to find out. Somehow, Aspen knew about the affair. She threatened to fill your husband in."

Maggie whispered, "How did you find out about that?"

Beatrice shook her head. "I can't tell you who told me. For obvious reasons."

"You mean because I'd end up killing your source?" Maggie gave a sharp laugh. "Then what makes you think I'm going to spare *you*? You also know about it."

Despite the way a chill went up her back at Maggie's words, Beatrice made sure her voice was level when she asked, "Did you do it? Did you kill Aspen to make sure she stayed silent about your affair? Or to stop her from blackmailing you?"

Maggie pulled her coat more tightly around her. She gave Beatrice a resentful look. "This is exactly why I didn't mention anything about my affair. I knew it was going to end up being misconstrued. Yes, I was relieved Aspen was gone. You don't know how excited I was when I heard the news."

"How did Aspen find out about your affair?"

"Who knows?" asked Maggie, rolling her eyes. "Aspen was like a witch. It seemed like she could find out everything about everybody. Maybe she had spies. Maybe she just kept her eyes and ears open. I know I was very careful, and I know the man I'm seeing was, too. How Aspen found out about the affair is a mystery to me."

"And she was blackmailing you?"

Maggie pressed her lips together before saying, "She was in the process of blackmailing me. She'd already made some leading statements like 'gosh, wouldn't it be terrible if James found out about your affair?' That kind of thing. Definitely toying with me. I was desperate to get her back. I was hoping to find something on Aspen. Something I could hold against her so that I could threaten her with exposure."

"Like her own affair?"

Maggie said, "That's the thing about Aspen—she simply didn't care. She didn't care if *everyone* knew about her affairs. It didn't bother her if her marriage fell apart or if she lost money or if people talked about her. She seemed to revel in it. Needless to say, I didn't have any luck getting dirt on her. I mean, dirt that she cared about, anyway."

"Could you have turned her into the police for blackmail? I have the feeling being deprived of her freedom and sent to prison might have given her pause," said Beatrice.

"Yes, but then *my* secret would be out. And that's precisely what I didn't want to happen, as Aspen knew. James can be heartless, and he'd have turned me out of our house and cut me off without a penny. Unfortunately, I'm not exactly rife with marketable skills." Maggie made a face. "And I don't think I want to go back home to live with my parents at my age."

"You've gotten used to a particular standard of living?"

"Sure! Of course I have. Nicole and I didn't come from a really lavish background, you know. Our dad was a school custodian and our mom cleaned houses. We had the basics, but it was no-frills. I wasn't particularly great at school, so I knew I wasn't going to be able to claw my way out of poverty with my brain. Nicole was a better student than I was, and she's made a nice living for herself. But it's not like she's making a ton of money. When I married James, I felt finally like I could breathe a little. The wolf wasn't at the door anymore."

"Were you happy with James?"

"It's been fine. I've been happy enough," said Maggie. "I know that's not a ringing endorsement, but I think happiness is overrated, in general. Contentedness is all you really need. I believe it's unrealistic to think a couple can be *happy* together for decades. I've never wanted to leave James. Let's put it that way. He's introduced me to a very comfortable lifestyle, apart from any worry. That's all that I've wanted."

Maggie must have been able to read Beatrice's mind because she added, "And maybe I also wanted a little diversion from reality. Which was really what my affair was all about."

Beatrice nodded. "So you're saying that, despite the motive being there, you had nothing to do with Aspen's death. Nor Olive's."

Maggie blanched at the mention of Olive. "No one could think I had anything to do with Olive's death. I had a great deal of respect for her. I'd never lay a finger on Olive. I can't wrap my head around why someone would murder her."

"Perhaps she saw or heard something that made her realize who'd killed Aspen." Beatrice paused. "And your sister?"

Maggie stared at her. "Nicole would never have harmed Aspen or Olive."

"What if she were trying to protect you? Can you see her deciding to get Aspen out of your way? It would have meant an end to your worries. The two of you seem very close."

Maggie said, "Well, of course we are! We're sisters. And yes, Nicole is very protective of me. But that protectiveness doesn't extend to murder. She's not exactly in the mafia or anything. Besides, Nicole never left the cabin the entire night."

Beatrice said slowly, "But you said you were a very heavy sleeper."

Maggie faltered a moment before quickly saying, "I meant that she and I were both sound asleep."

The door suddenly opened and Nicole was standing there, frowning. "What's going on? It sounds like Maggie is getting upset."

Maggie took one look at her sister and burst into tears. But Beatrice was wondering if it was because she'd been asked some pretty standard questions or whether it was from thinking Nicole could have had something to do with Aspen's murder. What if she had noticed Nicole getting up at night and leaving the cabin?

Maggie finally got control of herself and grabbed a tissue from a box on Starr's desk, dabbing her face with it. "Sorry," she muttered. "This place has me so stressed out. No heat, no lights, and a murderer on the loose. This is a disaster."

Nicole looked directly at Beatrice. "You can't possibly think Maggie had anything to do with this."

Beatrice said calmly, "I'm not thinking anything. I'm asking everyone questions to try to figure out what's going on. And hopefully prevent another death."

Maggie said to Nicole, "She knows about the blackmail. Somebody heard us talking about it." She turned back to Beatrice. "I know people sometimes talk about me. It doesn't mean anything."

"People are jealous of Maggie," said Nicole. "It must seem like she has a very easy life. But appearances are deceiving. She has a lot on her mind." Then Nicole seemed to make a decision. She said in a quiet voice, "I know you saw me leave the cabin last night, Maggie. Is that what's been worrying you?"

Maggie stared silently at her sister.

Nicole said, "I knew Aspen told the group she was going to do some late-night quilting. She was a night owl. I couldn't sleep. I was thinking about the blackmail and how stressed-out Maggie was. I figured it might be a good time to approach Aspen on her own and try to reason with her. But when I walked into the conference room, I found Aspen. She was already dead." Nicole now looked nervous and swallowed. "I didn't say anything because I was worried I'd be considered a suspect. I didn't touch anything, but went right back to my room."

Maggie and Beatrice just looked at her.

"It's the truth," said Nicole simply. "I'm sorry I didn't mention anything earlier. I just didn't want any of this stuff about Maggie's affair to get out."

Beatrice nodded. "Thanks for telling us now. Who do you think did do this?"

The two sisters started flinging names out. Basically, they thought it could be anyone but them.

They must have been able to read Beatrice's expression because they stopped. Nicole said a bit guiltily, "It's not that we really think they did it. We're just saying they *could* have done it. And they had a motive to do it. That's all."

Nicole and Maggie looked at each other, clearly eager to leave the office and Beatrice's probing questions. "I think that's all I've got," said Nicole. "I'm sorry I didn't say anything earlier."

Maggie said, "Yeah, you might have aged me a few years by staying quiet. I *knew* you couldn't possibly have been involved, but it sure made me worried. I didn't know why you'd gone out."

The sisters left, still talking with each other in low voices. Beatrice stood up, feeling suddenly exhausted. She hadn't really gotten any sleep the night before and it didn't look as if it was going to be a great night to catch up on missed sleep. If she'd had a hard time sleeping simply because she was in a different location, trying to rest in a room full of women while sleeping on the floor didn't seem promising.

When she got back to the main room of the lodge, it was a lot quieter in there than it had been earlier. A few women were talking desultorily in low voices to each other. A couple were trying to read, but kept looking up from their books. Cora from the Sew and Sews was working on some hand stitching. But the

Monopoly game had been put away, and the chatter had dissipated.

Piper gave her mother a smile as Beatrice took a seat next to her along the wall.

"How did everything go?" she asked quietly.

"It's going. It's kind of an awkward process. It's like I'm operating from the assumption that everyone is guilty until proven innocent instead of the other way around. But everyone is answering questions. I think I need to speak to Village Quilters for the next series of interviews."

Piper said, "Although none of them could have done it, of course."

"Of course. But they definitely could have seen or heard something that could help us out. Savannah has already been able to share some helpful observations. How is everything going here? It seems a lot more muted."

Piper nodded. "Things got a little ugly when Starr was explaining that she knew Aspen prior to this weekend. There were a lot of accusations being thrown around."

"It was something of a surprise," said Beatrice, making a face. "But the fact of the matter is that we really need Starr. She knows everything about this retreat. Plus, she lives within walking distance and can get her hands on extra supplies at home, if she needs to."

"That's what I kept saying to the group after Starr walked out. But the Sew and Sews were in a real snit about it. They've felt like they've all been under a cloud of suspicion. It must in some ways have been a relief to have someone else come up as a possible suspect."

Beatrice said, "Where is Starr now? She'd mentioned taking care of the food."

"She and Meadow headed off to the kitchen to see what they could do about feeding us. It seems like grilling for this number of people would take a while, and they're not even entirely sure that the grills would stay lit with the wind driving ice over the flames."

Beatrice said, "Maybe we should just plan on eating dry goods until the weather slows down a little. Has anybody been able to use a data signal to see a weather forecast?"

"Not as far as I know. Plus, everyone is pretty conservative about using their phones now that we can't recharge them. The power outage is creating lots of issues."

Beatrice said, "One of them is going to be staying warm. At least everyone seems to have brought good winter gear with them. But Starr was saying the firewood needs to be transported over to the lodge from a storage shed. Out in this weather, that could be tricky, especially since the sun is going down."

"I'll help out with the firewood. I'm one of the youngest people here. I wouldn't want anybody to break a hip in the wintry mix out there."

"Unfortunately, I think all of us might be susceptible to falling and there's really not much of a way to avoid it. Starr has been trying to take on everything herself, but she's obviously going to need some help since there's no staff here. I thought maybe we could divide up responsibilities with cooking and firewood. There might be other tasks, too, but I can't really think of them now."

Piper said sympathetically, "Because you're totally exhausted. I can see you're tapped out. You didn't get any sleep last night and then all this happened. Why don't you try to take a short nap?"

Beatrice shook her head. "I'd like to, but at this point it would probably only serve to mess up the sleep I get tonight. I should probably start interviewing the quilters again."

"Just give it a break for a short period," urged Piper. "Maybe read for a few minutes. You need to take care of yourself right now, too."

So Beatrice did. At first, she thought there was no way she'd be able to focus on a book with everything going on. But to her surprise, she felt herself being drawn right into the book she'd borrowed from Piper. She read until it was time to eat again.

The meal they all ended up eating wasn't exactly as tasty as what they'd eaten the day before. Meadow and Starr decided it would be quicker and easier to just serve everyone continental breakfast items for supper. As Meadow muttered to Beatrice, "We were worried about everybody getting in an even worse mood if we didn't hurry up and provide something to eat. And the last thing we need is to get a murderer fired up even more than they already are."

Piper did get firewood, with Starr's help. Then Meadow put out a signup sheet for women to sign up for various slots to do things like help with food prep or getting the firewood.

After eating, most everyone decided to call it a day, despite the early hour. It was already dark outside, and there wasn't enough light to see to read or really play a game, even if anyone had been in the right frame of mind to play. They trooped over to the cabins in groups for pillows and blankets and settled into a rather uncomfortable sleep.

Chapter Fourteen

At first, Beatrice was certain she wasn't going to be able to sleep a wink, especially with Miss Sissy's snoring practically raising the rafters in the lodge. But then her absolute exhaustion caught up with her and she drifted into a deep sleep.

She awoke with a start the next morning. Miss Sissy was staring grumpily at her. Beatrice gave her a questioning look, and the old woman made a motion to indicate eating. Beatrice raised herself onto her elbows and looked around the room. Everyone appeared to be still sacked out. Meadow was snoring gently.

Beatrice nodded at Miss Sissy and got up as quietly as she could. This wasn't an easy task with the room being as chilly as it was and the fact that she'd slept on the floor. Her joints felt stiff, and she told herself that once she got into the dining hall, she'd do some stretching. There certainly wasn't enough space in the lodge to stretch.

As Beatrice put her heavy coat on, she noticed wryly that Miss Sissy seemed just as spry as ever. She wasn't sure exactly how old she was. Twenty years older than Beatrice? More? She'd like to know her secret.

Miss Sissy rapidly piled a weathered-looking winter gear on and headed for the door. When they opened it, snow blew in as well as a frigid gust of air. She saw a couple of women wake briefly and lifted a hand in apology. Then she and Miss Sissy headed outside. Or, rather, directly into the snowdrift that had formed outside the lodge door.

Miss Sissy said, "Bah!" and kicked at the snow.

"At least it's not ice," offered Beatrice. She looked at the sky. "And maybe it's slowing down. Come on, let's get something to eat."

She was rather surprised the old woman hadn't set out on her own to get food. Maybe Miss Sissy could read her thoughts because she snarled, "Buddy system." It was true. Besides, if Miss Sissy wasn't monitored, it was entirely possible that she would wipe out much of the food supply.

It was the first time Beatrice had really taken a look inside the retreat kitchen. There was a large, well-stocked pantry, which relieved Beatrice, although Starr had definitely insisted that there was plenty of food. Still, it was nice to see it for herself. There were also a couple of industrial-sized refrigerators, which Beatrice presumed were empty since Starr had said she was going to put everything in coolers and out in the cold to keep the food from going bad during the power outage.

"Let's see," said Beatrice, peering at the contents of the pantry. "There's some cereal here. How about dry cereal?"

Miss Sissy stared at her in disbelief. "Had that for supper!"

"Well, it doesn't feel as if we have a lot of options here, considering we don't have any power."

"Eggs. Eggs are easy."

Beatrice felt as if her patience might be petering out. "Eggs are easy when you have power. Eggs are hard when you don't."

"Oatmeal."

Beatrice said, "Oatmeal requires hot water. Hot water requires power."

"Boil it on the grill."

Beatrice shook her head. "Not with the way the wind is blowing snow and ice everywhere. Plus, I'm not the world's most experienced griller. I'd just end up using up the charcoal and not delivering hot water. No, I'm not doing anything with the grill."

The old woman was looking belligerent now, and Beatrice sighed. "Let's see what else is available."

They poked around the large pantry, with Miss Sissy growling at the dry goods from time to time.

"Yogurt!" Miss Sissy finally demanded.

Beatrice could tell it was something of a concession. It wasn't dry cereal, but it wasn't eggs or oatmeal either.

"Okay. I have the feeling a place like this would probably have had yogurt as an offering. But Starr put all the contents of the fridges outside to keep them from going bad. I'm guessing the coolers might be covered with snow."

Miss Sissy held up her hands, which were encased in what appeared to be handmade gloves.

"You'll dig them out? Okay. I definitely admire your determination. Let's see if we can find them."

It was strangely disorienting outdoors. The pure whiteness of everything in the early morning light was not only eerie, but it also made it hard to know exactly where you were. "Let's stay close to each other," urged Beatrice.

Miss Sissy gave her a baleful look before glancing quickly around her, eyes narrowed as she searched for anything that might resemble coolers. She seized on one likely snow-covered shape and started digging. She hissed when she saw it was only a tree stump.

"What about this?" asked Beatrice, gesturing to another snowy apparition. She helped Miss Sissy dig and soon they uncovered a red-topped cooler. Miss Sissy yanked the top off and looked hungrily inside. Then she gave a scornful snort.

Beatrice peered in. "Nothing really edible here, is there? Unless you were desperate."

Miss Sissy's glare seemed to indicate that it would be a while before she stooped to consume butter, mustard, and other condiments.

The old woman looked fiercely around, undeterred by the snow flying into her eyes, until her gaze settled on another lump in the snow. She started burrowing right away and Beatrice helped her.

This time, they uncovered something a bit better. There were cheeses in there and milk. Apparently satisfied, at least for right then, Miss Sissy grabbed them and started hurrying back to the dining hall, likely to allow the cereal to be reunited with the milk. Beatrice was just glad they were heading inside the building. She felt as if she were turning into an ice cube.

Miss Sissy headed back for the kitchen and put her bounty down on a prep table. Beatrice said, "Hey, that milk is probably frozen. You might want to give it some time."

The old woman glared at her. But she soon discovered the truth in Beatrice's words. The milk was basically a milk popsicle. The cheeses were very hard, too. Miss Sissy gave a frustrated snort.

"You felt that wind. Even if we can light the grill, it's going to get extinguished. I know you're hungry. We'll just have to wait." Beatrice paused. "Also, it might be a good idea to pace yourself, in terms of eating. We don't want any bad feelings from the other women. There's probably a limited amount of 'tasty' food."

Miss Sissy clearly wasn't too fond of that idea. She sat herself down on a stool and watched the cheese and milk as if her scowl alone might melt it.

A few minutes later the doors to the dining hall opened up and Starr and Nicole appeared. Starr spotted them and looked relieved. "Oh good. I thought one or two guests might be missing when I woke up."

"Everything okay?" asked Nicole.

Beatrice nodded. "Miss Sissy woke up hungry, and we thought we'd forage for food."

"There's plenty of dry cereal," said Starr.

Miss Sissy made a face. "Blechh."

Nicole blinked at her and Beatrice hid a smile.

"We're just waiting for some of our finds to defrost a little," said Beatrice.

Starr bobbed her head briskly. "Fine. Nicole and I were going to find ourselves something to eat before we headed off to my house."

"Are you sure that's still a good idea?" asked Beatrice. "The weather has taken another turn, as I'm sure you noticed on your way here from the lodge. The wind is pretty fierce. Plus, the snow is on top of a layer of ice. How far are you talking about walking?"

Starr made a dismissive gesture. "It's just something like half a mile." She pulled out a large container of cereal and two bowls.

Miss Sissy growled at this. Nicole stared at her again.

Beatrice said, "That would be a piece of cake under ordinary circumstances. But it sure isn't now. That snow is going to take a long while to wade through. And I feel half-frozen, although Miss Sissy and I weren't even out there very long."

Nicole said, "Regardless, we're going to give it a shot. Maybe we can even get a cell phone signal at Starr's house. Right now, we're all like sitting ducks. And I, for one, don't like feeling that way. I want to *do* something."

Starr shoved a bowl of cornflakes and a spoon at her. "That's what we'll do. Just as soon as we eat something."

Nicole sighed. "I guess it's too much to ask to get a coffee."

Beatrice said, "I'm missing it, too. But I just don't think the grills are going to operate in these conditions. Even to boil a pot of water."

The door to the dining hall opened, and Posy peered inside. Her anxious expression relaxed as soon as she spotted the other women. "Oh, thank heavens. I woke up and had this horrible idea that maybe Miss Sissy had gone missing and the rest of you were out looking for her."

Miss Sissy looked intrigued by this idea.

Starr shook her head. "No. Believe me, I'd wake everybody up if anyone disappeared. We'd figure out a way to look." She glanced over at Nicole, who had eaten most of her cereal. "We should probably head out in a minute. The weather might even deteriorate."

"From this? This is pretty bad." Now Nicole looked a little uncertain.

"Are you sure you're going to be able to find your way?" asked Posy. "The snow is blanketing everything so much. I think I'd get really disoriented."

"It should be fine. I've walked the path a hundred times or more. Even if the landscape looks different, I should be good to make it home by pure muscle memory."

Several minutes later, Starr and Nicole bundled back up and headed out into the swirling snow.

Posy said uneasily, "I'm worried about them. Maybe I should have gone with them."

Miss Sissy made a scoffing sound. Beatrice said, "I'm with Miss Sissy. Those two were eager to take on the challenge. It doesn't mean anyone else needs to be endangered."

Miss Sissy picked up one of the cheeses and banged it with frustration onto the table. Beatrice and Posy looked ruefully at each other and opened the container of cornflakes.

Beatrice said, "Since we're alone now, except for Miss Sissy, do you think you could talk about yesterday? I'm going to try to speak with a few Village Quilters this morning before I tackle another interview with any of the Sew and Sews."

Posy nodded, swallowing down a spoonful of dry cereal with some difficulty. "Sure. I've been thinking about it over and over. Maybe it will help me to tell you about it."

Beatrice gave her a hopeful look. "Does that mean you might know something?"

Posy shook her head sadly. "I wish I did. But unless I'm missing something, I don't believe I do."

Posy recounted her previous day. She was pretty much on the outskirts of the Sew and Sews instead of interacting with them. She said Meadow had been more sociable and that Beatrice should make sure to ask Meadow her impressions of the women.

Beatrice sighed. "I already have. Meadow, of course, thought they were great. They're quilters, after all."

Posy gave a fond smile. "That sounds like Meadow. Anyway, that's pretty much my day. I don't think I have a lot to offer. Aspen seemed like a handful. And Olive, to me, looked desperately unhappy. Aside from that, those were my only real recollections."

Miss Sissy looked decidedly unimpressed with Posy's offerings.

Posy turned to the old woman. "What did you think of everyone?"

Miss Sissy made a growling noise.

Beatrice wondered if she needed a warmup question first. "How about their quilting? Did you see any of the projects they were working on?"

Miss Sissy looked a bit more receptive to this question. "Pretty good stuff," she muttered.

Posy nodded. "I thought the same thing. They looked like they were the kind of guild that liked pushing each other to do better and try new things."

Beatrice grinned at her. "It's a lovely thought, but I think we're all sort of stuck in our routines, aren't we? I can't imagine convincing Savannah to switch over from geometric prints."

"Yes, but when she got Meadow's crazy quilt when we did a swap, she did a great job with it. I just don't think she'd be happy doing that on a regular basis."

Beatrice said, "Right. Or, for that matter, if we tried to force Meadow into making geometric patterns. She'd get bored so fast, it would end up as a UFO in no time."

UFOs were unfinished objects in the quilting world. Beatrice had collected quite a few of them herself.

Miss Sissy, apparently now more in a mood to talk, despite the fact that her unsatiated appetite was making her grouchy, muttered, "Cranky."

"*You're* cranky?" asked Posy.

Miss Sissy scowled at her. "No!"

Beatrice thought the old woman protested too much.

"Who's cranky?" asked Posy.

"The dead woman."

"Which dead woman?" asked Beatrice.

Miss Sissy stared at them both as if they were stupid. "The second one!"

Beatrice said, "Hmm. I felt the same thing. Not that she was cranky, but that she seemed really distracted and removed. Neither of you happened to see her speaking with someone one-on-one, did you?"

They both considered this and shook their heads.

Beatrice sighed. "Okay. Well, it was worth a try."

The door to the dining hall opened once again, and Ivy stumbled in, snow in her hair and even stuck to her eyelashes.

Unfortunately, she seemed about as grouchy as Miss Sissy was. Beatrice was sure the lack of hot food would put the hungry quilters in a much poorer mood than they otherwise would have been.

"Where is everybody?" Ivy asked as she came in. "Shouldn't Nicole be in here? And Starr?"

"They've set off for Starr's house," said Posy, still looking worried.

Ivy made a face. "In this weather? Better them than me. I don't know what they're really going to accomplish except getting frostbite."

Frostbite didn't look as if it were going to be an issue for Ivy. She'd brought most of her bedding with her and it was wrapped around her like a toga. As well, she was in a thick coat, gloves, and hat.

Beatrice said slowly, "I've just finished speaking with Posy and Miss Sissy. Could I speak with you, too, Ivy? Since you're here, anyway?"

Chapter Fifteen

Ivy looked as if this didn't entirely suit, but like she couldn't immediately think of a way to get out of it. "I guess so, if you really have to talk with everybody. But I don't know anything, so it's definitely not going to be worth your time."

Miss Sissy hit the cheese against the table again, looking at it with disgust.

"How about if we move over here where we can talk quietly?" asked Beatrice, motioning to a far corner of the room.

Ivy said quickly, "I'll join you as soon as I've gotten something to eat. Do we have any pastries? Fresh bread?"

Miss Sissy stared at her as if Ivy had suddenly suggested the abominable snowman had entered the dining hall. She slammed the cheese against the table again, as if to make a point.

Beatrice shook her head. "Not that we've been able to uncover. We've all been eating from that container of cornflakes."

So a few minutes later, a sulky-looking Ivy sat across from Beatrice. She had a small bowl of cereal and looked at it with distaste. Aside from Ivy's general peevishness, Beatrice noticed that the woman's face was rather drawn and her color was poor. All-in-all, she looked as if she were feeling ill. She remembered Cora saying earlier that Ivy was rather delicate. She certainly looked fragile now.

"Are you all right?" asked Beatrice.

Ivy shrugged. "I guess I'm doing about the same as everybody else right now. I just want to go home. That's all I can think about. I slept horribly last night and from what I can see, tonight isn't going to be any better. I ate dry cereal last night and I'm eating it again this morning. Life isn't fun right now."

"I understand that," said Beatrice. "Unfortunately, there really isn't anything we can do."

"I can think of one thing I could do. I could set out on foot, head to the road, and flag somebody down. That would be something."

Beatrice shook her head. "With the snow drifting the way it is, there's no way now to even be able to tell where the road is. Plus, the likelihood of anybody driving is very low. There wouldn't be anyone to flag down."

Ivy slumped in her chair, poking at her cornflakes with her spoon. "I guess. I've just never been so miserable and unhappy in my life." She paused. "Poor Olive. She didn't deserve what happened to her."

"And Aspen did?" asked Beatrice without judgment.

Ivy made a face. "I'm not saying that. Not totally. But Aspen deserved it more than Olive did, that's for sure. And before you ask, no. No, I didn't have an alibi. But I also didn't kill her."

Beatrice's head started hurting just a bit. It seemed that, despite all the enforced togetherness of the group yesterday, no one had really paid any attention to anyone's comings or goings.

Ivy continued, almost echoing Beatrice's own thoughts. "I was with people. But then I wandered off to go to the restroom or back to my cabin to grab something. Then I would go get a snack or try to make a call again. No one was paying any attention to where people were."

"You did go back to your cabin?"

"I sure did," said Ivy a bit belligerently. "And if others tell you they didn't, they're lying. I felt like escaping from everybody. My nerves can't handle this kind of pressure. And yes, I wanted to grab a few things there to take back with me to the lodge, but I also spent time putting my feet up and reflecting. Just getting away from people. Don't you ever feel that way?"

Beatrice could certainly relate. In fact, she often felt the need to get away from others and that need was growing the longer this situation was going on. She gave a little nod. "You mentioned others were going back to their cabins, too. Do you remember who you saw?"

Ivy blew out a breath. "Well, I saw lots of folks from your guild. That weird old woman, for one."

Clearly Miss Sissy.

Ivy said, "She looks like she has murder on the brain all the time, frankly. She was worrying me while she was slamming that block of cheese on the table. That frozen cheese would make a pretty effective murder weapon."

"Anyone else?" asked Beatrice.

"Yes. A woman from your group who looks like she needs a makeover. She's thin with heavy eyebrows."

Obviously, a description of Savannah.

"Got it," said Beatrice. She paused. "How about any of the Sew and Sews?"

Ivy glared at her. "I see how it is. So you're just going to dismiss the fact that I saw a bunch of Village Quilters roaming around at the time of the murder."

"No. But you've got to understand that there isn't any reason for women from our group to murder Aspen or Olive. We didn't even meet them until yesterday. And I can promise you that none of these women are homicidal maniacs."

Ivy shot her a doubtful look. "Well, that old woman sure seems to be. And we were saying Starr didn't know anybody either, and look how wrong we were about that. I'm going to reserve judgement, and I think you should, too. If you're going to play this role, you need to be able to keep the open mind that goes along with it."

As much as it irritated Beatrice, she knew Ivy was right. "Okay. Did you see anyone else?"

Ivy sighed. "Yeah. I saw Maggie. Then I saw Nicole *looking* for Maggie. Then I saw Cora."

Beatrice knit her brows. "How much time did you spend outside?"

"Oh no, I could see everyone from the window of the cabin. No, I spend as little time as possible outside in this weather. That's why the retreat should refund us our money. The whole idea was to spend time in nature and relax."

Ivy was looking querulous again, and Beatrice interjected before she could start another rant on how the weekend had gone so very wrong. "What did you think about Olive?"

"I liked her. She was organized and dedicated to the guild. Whenever we needed volunteers for something, she was always the first one who raised her hand. She was a good leader, too. And she often did tasks no one else wanted to do. I mean, Olive wasn't the most fun-loving person. She wasn't someone you'd call up for lunch or to come over and have a few drinks and dish on people. But she was super-responsible and trustworthy."

"Unlike Aspen," said Beatrice.

"Totally unlike Aspen in every single way," agreed Ivy. "But although Aspen could be fun, she was completely unenjoyable to be around because she stressed everybody out. She was always looking for a way to get at you." She made a face. "When I spent that quiet time in my cabin yesterday, I got to thinking. I was being pretty reactive in my feelings toward Aspen. The fact of the matter is that she did me something of a favor."

"Did she?"

Ivy nodded. "Because of her, I realized what a despicable man my husband was. When I'd confronted Aspen over her affair with my husband, she told me that she was far from the first person he'd had an affair with."

"That must have been hurtful."

Ivy said, "Of course it was. That's exactly why she said it. But the fact of the matter was that it was all true. Like I said, in some ways she did me a favor. The last thing I wanted was to be in blissful ignorance and have everybody in town pitying me because I was the only one who didn't know."

Beatrice wasn't sure what to say, so it was a good thing Ivy continued. "I'd thought this retreat was going to give me time to figure out what to do. And I guess it has. I thought I could decide whether I should stay with my husband, forgive him, and look like the bigger person, or whether I should leave him and get a nice settlement in the divorce. Now I realize life's too short. Life's too short to live with a guy like that. I don't trust him at all anymore. Whenever he left the house, I'd be wondering if he was telling me the truth about where he was going. I can't live like that."

"I don't really know you or the situation, but it sounds like that might be a good plan," said Beatrice.

Ivy nodded, still deep in her own thoughts and almost as if she'd forgotten Beatrice was even there. "That's right. I'll set up my own place and do what *I* want to do for once." She looked at Beatrice. "He wasn't that great of a guy, anyway. He was always critical of me. He'd point out if I'd gained a little weight and make snide jokes about it. Appearances are everything to him. Really, like I said, Aspen did me a favor."

Beatrice said, "Getting back to her murder, I'm thinking it must still all go back to whoever killed Aspen. That person would have probably murdered Olive to cover up the crime. It seems as though Olive must have known something. While you were thinking things over yesterday afternoon, did you have any more ideas about who might have done this?"

"I don't *know* anything. All I can do is speculate. But one thing I kept thinking about is my husband's interest in appearances. That made me start thinking about Maggie. I know you don't know her very well, but she's always obsessed with how she presents herself to the world."

Beatrice thought about Maggie's wearing a fur coat and matching hat at a quilting retreat. She nodded. "So you're thinking Maggie might have murdered Aspen in order to keep her life the way it is? To manage appearances?"

Ivy shrugged. "Maybe. Who knows? I'm simply thinking Maggie has a lot to lose. She has this rich husband who *also* cares a lot about appearances. I know about her affair. I saw her steal a kiss from the guy when she thought nobody was around. I thought it was really foolish of her at the time, considering she's married to a man who'd divorce her at the drop of a hat."

"And you think Aspen knew about this? Maggie's affair?" Beatrice knew Aspen did, of course. But she thought that Maggie's affair should probably be kept under wraps. She was curious to know who else knew about it.

"Sure. If I could find out about Maggie's affair, someone like Aspen definitely could. Aspen was a total snoop. And she wasn't only a snoop, she was someone who actively looked for the kind of dirt she could use against you."

Beatrice asked, "You mean for blackmail?"

"I don't know if she blackmailed people or if she just taunted them with stuff she'd found out. Either way, it would have been bad. Maybe she told Maggie she was going to let her husband know about Maggie's affair. Just to be mean. That's the way she was. And now, if that's all you've got, I'd like to go back to the lodge with my little bowl of cornflakes and wallow in my unhappiness."

Beatrice watched Ivy stomp off.

Posy came over, looking sympathetic. "How did that go?"

"Well, I think it's been reinforced numerous times that Aspen was not a very nice person," said Beatrice with a sigh. "Although everyone seemed to like Olive, even though she wasn't perhaps the life of the party. But she was the kind of person who got stuff done."

Posy gave her a smile. "Just in case no one has done it yet, I wanted to thank you for taking the time to do this. I appreciate what you're doing to try to get to the bottom of this and to keep us all safe."

It was just like Posy to be sweet like that. Beatrice smiled back at her. "Thanks. I'm not sure I'm getting any closer to an answer, but I'm giving it a go. I have to justify Meadow's faith in me you know."

They both chuckled at that. To hear Meadow, you'd think Beatrice worked for the FBI.

Beatrice said, "How are *you* doing? This has been hard on everyone. How are you holding up so far?"

Posy looked wistful. "I'm okay. I just wish I could get in touch with Cork."

Cork was Posy's husband. He owned a very popular wine store in downtown Dappled Hills and was as gruff as Posy was gentle. But the two seemed very close with each other and had recently taken to traveling.

"I know you must miss him."

"Like you miss Wyatt. It's especially hard knowing how worried they must be about us all. At least Meadow was able to get through briefly to Ramsay. I'm sure he let all our husbands know we're okay."

Beatrice nodded. "It's probably best she didn't have the chance to tell him there'd been a murder. They would be even more worried about us then."

"It would be good to be able to bounce all this off of Cork, too, though. Cork always makes me feel safe. I don't feel especially safe right now." Posy stopped and gave Beatrice a rueful look. "Sorry. I'm pointing out the obvious and probably not helping your stress levels, either."

"I think talking about it *does* help, actually. This weekend has been a lot to process."

Posy said, "I feel like everyone is just so aimless right now. Maybe we can do some group quilting to try to alleviate that. I know a lot of our supplies are in the conference room with Aspen, but maybe we have enough, collectively, to be able to work on our quilts."

"You're right. Love of quilting is what brought us together in the first place. It seems right that it would help give us some direction through this."

Posy nodded. "I know you're busy helping figure out what's going on. I'll see if I can drum up some interest in quilting when everyone is up for the day. Plus, we all like to chat when we're working together. Maybe I can glean information that could be useful."

Beatrice smiled at her. "Great idea all round, Posy."

Posy said, "I was so looking forward to this weekend, too. Now I feel like Edgenora and June Bug were lucky not to be able to come." She shook her head. "I need to focus on all the positives of the weekend."

"Which are?" Beatrice lifted an eyebrow.

Posy seemed at a loss. Then she smiled. "Well, it hasn't been boring."

"That's for sure." They grinned at each other.

Meadow's voice boomed out. "Why the sunny faces? Were you able to call out?"

Meadow walked over to them with Miss Sissy in tow. The old woman clearly didn't want to let Meadow out of her sight.

Beatrice shook her head. "Nothing that exciting. Posy and I were just cheering each other up."

"Well, I'm going to work on a way to cheer us up some more. I'll try to tackle that grill."

"Will you?" asked Beatrice. The idea of having something, anything, hot fairly made her mouth water. "Do you think you can? We're not at all sure that the grill can even function with all the snow blowing and the gales of wind."

Miss Sissy growled and gave Beatrice a warning look which she interpreted as a fierce request to avoid dissuading Meadow from trying.

Meadow shrugged. "It might be tricky. But I want to try. There's not a lot to do around here."

"Got it. I can show you where those coolers were outside."

The idea of going back out into the whirling snow wasn't particularly appealing. Meadow might have picked up on this because she shook her head. "I'll find them, thanks. You just worry about solving these murders." Meadow swept off. This time, Miss Sissy stayed put. Maybe she didn't fancy going out into the snowy maelstrom again, either.

"I feel as if we're in great hands," said Posy, looking relieved. "You'll figure out what's going on here. Meadow is on cooking duty."

"And you'll help foster some good feelings with quilting," said Beatrice.

Posy stood up. "I think I'll check in at the lodge. Surely everyone must be stirring over there. It might be a relief for the women to at least have something on the agenda for the day."

After Posy left, Miss Sissy and Beatrice were left staring at each other. Beatrice smiled at her. "Doing okay, Miss Sissy?" she asked lightly.

Miss Sissy gave her a disgusted look as if Beatrice should have known better than to even ask the question.

"Don't like it," she snarled.

"I know. I'm sorry the fun weekend we planned got scuttled. And sorry you missed out on your s'mores."

The old woman glared at her. "Might still have s'mores."

Beatrice had the feeling that s'mores had slipped down some on the list of priorities. "Maybe."

Miss Sissy growled, "Don't like it. People fighting. People dying."

Beatrice frowned at her. "People fighting? You mean arguing?"

"Bah. Fussing at each other."

Beatrice asked, "Like who?"

"That Olive."

"Olive was arguing with someone? That could be important, Miss Sissy. Do you remember who she was arguing with? Did it look like a serious argument? Can you describe the woman?"

Chapter Sixteen

Miss Sissy narrowed her eyes at Beatrice.

"Sorry," said Beatrice. "Too many questions at once. Can you describe the woman Olive was arguing with?"

Miss Sissy glanced over at the cheese, still slowly defrosting on a nearby table.

"That cheese is going to take a while to defrost," said Beatrice.

Miss Sissy sighed. "Tired-looking."

That could describe most of the women in the group, including all the Village Quilters. Beatrice prodded a bit more. "Tired. Okay. Was she one of the younger Sew and Sews? Or one of the older ones?"

Miss Sissy was looking more distracted now, perhaps thinking about the food Meadow was going to try to grill. She tried to pull her attention back to the task at hand. "Middle."

The age sounded about right for Ivy, as did the tiredness. Beatrice asked, "Is she pretty?"

Miss Sissy gave her a canny look. "Used to be."

Definitely Ivy then. "Did you hear what they were arguing about? It could be important."

"Don't know," muttered Miss Sissy.

"Was it something about Aspen? Did the name Aspen come up?"

Miss Sissy's eyes narrowed even more. "Don't *know*."

Beatrice could tell she wasn't going to get anything else from the old woman. "Do you want to head over to the lodge with me? You probably need to warm up in front of the fire for a while. I know I do. I can give you a hand to make sure you don't fall down outside. It might be slick under the snow."

Miss Sissy shook her head violently. "Food."

"You've been up for a while. Why not just eat some of those cornflakes until Meadow can make something a little more filling?"

Judging from the sound coming from Miss Sissy, this suggestion was anathema to her, to say the least. Beatrice stood, bundling herself back up into her many layers and headed out into what felt like a snow globe, except with more wind.

Everyone was indeed stirring now. Many of the women had tidied up their bedding so that there was more room to walk through the room. The current conversation seemed focused on whether taking a hot shower was possible. The consensus was that it was powered by gas.

Posy had also clearly mentioned stockpiling quilting fabric and supplies because there was some chatter about that, too.

While the lively discussion continued, Beatrice quietly approached Ivy. "Could I speak with you for just a second?"

Ivy rolled her eyes. "I just spoke to you, you know."

"Yes. But there's one more thing I need to ask you about."

"Go ahead," said Ivy, looking annoyed.

"Let's talk in the office if you don't mind. It's more private thcre."

Ivy continued looking annoyed, but sighed in a resigned manner and stood up.

Just then, however, the door to the lodge opened and Nicole stood there, looking half frozen. Her eyelashes had snow stuck on them and she wiped her eyes off with an equally frozen coat sleeve. “I need help!” she called.

Chapter Seventeen

The roomful of women stood up. "What's wrong?" asked Posy anxiously.

"It's Starr. She's hurt. I don't have the strength to help her hobble here anymore so I ran to get you. Come on! I'll show you where she is."

"We don't all need to go," said Beatrice as the women all rushed to the door. "It's dangerous out there. Clearly."

Piper said, "I'll go." She looked at Georgia, who was equally young. "Want to come with me?"

Georgia nodded. They put on their coats, gloves, and hats and headed out with Nicole.

Posy said quietly, "I wonder what happened."

"She probably fell," said Beatrice grimly. "I noticed there was more ice coming down out there, which would've made the surface of the snow very slick. I wouldn't be surprised if she broke something."

A silence fell across the room, although it hadn't exactly been noisy before.

Posy started pulling on her coat. "I should make something warm for them drink."

"I'll help you," said Beatrice quickly. She couldn't stand sitting in the lodge doing nothing, especially with her daughter outside. It made her feel very antsy.

Back in the dining hall, Posy filled up a pot with water and Beatrice found some hot chocolate packets. They took them over to where Meadow was battling with the weather and the grill.

Meadow saw the pot and said, "Did something happen?"

"Starr got hurt during her trip home. We thought we'd make her a hot drink," said Posy.

"And Nicole looks half-frozen, too," said Beatrice. "Is the grill staying lit?"

"Intermittently," said Meadow. But her eyes had a determined gleam in them that Beatrice recognized. She'd bet on Meadow's ability to keep the fire going long enough to heat the water.

Beatrice and Posy stood where Meadow asked them to in order to block the wind a bit. The wind seemed to have a mind of its own, however, as it blew in a multitude of directions. Meadow put the pot of water on the grill and somehow made room for a small iron skillet. She looked so fierce that Beatrice decided the wind wouldn't dare impede her efforts.

Sure enough, soon after there were scrambled eggs and some very hot cups of hot chocolate.

"I'm on a roll," said Meadow grimly. "I'll stay here and keep cooking while the conditions are decent. Maybe we can all have some hot food or at least a hot drink.

Beatrice put the plates and cups on a tray Meadow had found in the pantry and hurried off toward the lodge.

Piper, Georgia, Nicole, and Starr arrived at the same time Beatrice did. Starr's face was pale as the snow they were treading on, and she was biting her lips so hard it was a wonder she wasn't making them bleed.

"You're going to be just fine," said Georgia in a comforting voice as she and Piper balanced Starr's weight between them with their arms around her. "One little hop at a time."

"We'll get you settled by the fire," said Piper to Starr. She gave Beatrice a weary smile.

"I've got scrambled eggs for Nicole and Starr. And hot chocolate, too. Meadow plans to see if we can all get some," said Beatrice.

Starr's eyes filled with tears, which she hastily blinked away. She nodded, and then took the remaining hops into the lodge.

Someone had pushed a recliner that had been along the wall in front of the fire, and Starr sank gratefully into it.

"Does anybody have a medical background?" asked Piper.

They looked around at each other, but no one did.

"Who has the *most* medical experience?" asked Beatrice.

Unfortunately, it appeared that two women were tied with lifeguard experience decades ago.

"What do you think might be wrong, Starr?" asked Beatrice instead.

"My legs. I slipped on a patch of ice and fell really oddly. It feels as if both legs are broken," grated Starr. Her face was still pale with pain, despite being in front of the warmth of the fire.

Not knowing what else to do, Beatrice shoved a cup of hot chocolate and a plate of food at her and then served Nicole, too. Nicole also seemed to be trying to defrost.

Piper said, "We should probably try to take a look at your injuries, shouldn't we? Make sure there isn't any bleeding we can stop?"

Beatrice nodded. "That's a good idea. And splints . . . shouldn't we make splints to try to keep her legs immobilized?"

Savannah said, "What can we use to make splints? Are there any planks or wood buried in snow right now?"

"Maybe a rolled-up blanket?" suggested Posy.

"We need to use all of those blankets for warmth," said Maggie.

Starr was still shivering. "There might be some extra bed slats in storage." She put her coffee cup down and pulled up her yoga pants as far as she could so they could take a look at her legs.

Beatrice winced. She was far from an expert, but both legs certainly seemed broken. And hugely swollen.

Beatrice stood up. "I'll see if I can find the bed slats."

"I'll help you," said Posy and Piper at once.

Posy said to Piper, "You just went out to help—you need to warm back up. I'll go along with Beatrice."

Maggie said, "Well, for my part, I'm going to see if I can reach somebody, anybody, who can get on the road and help us. Have we even reported a second death?"

"No one has been able to get through to anyone. Plus, our phones are going to be dead if we keep trying," said Ivy. "I don't want to use up any of my battery to try to call out when it's clearly pointless."

"My phone was almost fully charged when the power went off, so I'll try," said Maggie.

Posy and Beatrice headed back outside. Posy added, "I guess we need to find something to tie the slats to Starr's legs." She gave an anxious sigh.

"We'll find something," said Beatrice, wanting to reassure her. "This place is big, and I know they have all kinds of equipment to manage it. We'll be okay."

They got to the storage building and were momentarily overwhelmed. It was a big metal facility and was packed full of things. Perhaps the stuff in there was organized in a particular way to make it easier to find, but for the life of her, Beatrice couldn't figure out what that method was.

It was also very dark. There was a light switch on the wall which Beatrice had automatically reached for. Naturally, nothing happened.

Posy said, "I wish it at least had windows. Natural light would help a lot."

"Right now, I just feel lucky that we could open the door at all. The snow really isn't helping."

"Look—there's a shovel. Maybe we can clear around the door a little and let more light in," said Posy.

They took turns because the shoveling, even the little they needed to do, was exhausting. The icy snow was heavy, and both women were puffing with exertion as they went. But finally, they were able to clear enough of an opening for the door to open to its fullest extent.

"Need any help?" asked a voice behind them.

Beatrice gave Piper a rueful look. "You were supposed to be warming up inside."

Piper grinned at her mother. "I'm all warmed up. I got so warm that I decided I'd cool down again." She looked inside the storage building and made a face. "Kind of dark in there." She held out a couple of flashlights.

It was almost as if Piper were handing out diamonds and rubies. Beatrice and Posy couldn't have been more pleased. "Where did you find these?" asked Beatrice.

"Starr directed me to the dining hall. There were flashlights in the pantry there. Let's find ourselves some bed slats."

So they split up and peered through the dimness of the storage building. Posy called out, "Found them!" a few minutes later.

Beatrice looked at them. "Those are going to have to be trimmed down. They're far too long."

Piper said, "I spotted an axe somewhere in here."

She found it again, and they cut the slats to a more manageable length.

"Now let's get out of here," said Piper as another icy gale blew through the building. "We need to get warmed up."

"First, we should find some ties to lace the slats onto Starr," said Beatrice.

They poked around in the darkness a while longer until they found some rope of various lengths.

"Well, it won't be the most comfortable thing in the world, but hopefully it will work," said Beatrice.

They returned to the lodge where Starr was looking slightly better. At least, her color was better than it had been before. She brightened a little when she saw the slats and rope.

"Success, then," said Starr, breathing a sigh of relief.

"With the help of the flashlights," said Posy with a smile.

"Any luck calling out?" asked Beatrice.

Maggie shook her head. "Nope. It acted as if it wanted to connect once, but it didn't go through. I'll try again later."

They attached the slats to Starr's legs to form splints, then made her as comfortable as possible. Meadow, who'd finished up at the grill, had saved plates and hot drinks for Beatrice, Posy, and Piper. They ate and drank them contentedly. Or, as contentedly as it was possible to be.

"The cooking didn't take you as long as I thought it would," said Beatrice to Meadow.

"Oh, I had a sous-chef."

Meadow smiled at Savannah who looked pleased at the recognition. Beatrice was glad it was Savannah. She'd been worried for a second it might have been Miss Sissy, who would surely have eaten most of the foods she'd have been preparing.

"How are we doing with firewood?" asked Beatrice.

Cora said, "We've pulled some out from the woodpile and put it under a covering to dry a little. We do have some dry wood still available for later."

"Okay, good. I'll grab some when the fire in here starts getting low," said Beatrice.

"Or I will," interjected Piper. "Why don't you go put your feet up for a while? You've been doing a lot."

Beatrice's first instinct was to turn her down. Then, suddenly, she felt very, very tired. It must suddenly be hitting her—all the stress and the worry. Trying to figure out how to make the best of a bad situation. "Actually, I think I'll take you up on that."

"The bedding is all piled up on the side," said Maggie, nodding to the stacks of rolled up blankets and pillows.

Although she knew they were making a point of staying together, the thought of lying down in the middle of all the activity in the lodge was not very appealing. To fully recharge, as she felt she needed to recharge, it meant withdrawing for a little while.

"I think I'll head to the cabin. I could really do with stretching out and having some space."

Meadow said, "But it's freezing there!"

"I can bring blankets with me. And I'll stay in my coat and hat." Everyone still looked worried, so Beatrice added, "I won't be there for long. Just long enough to take a little nap."

"How about if I come, too?" asked Piper.

Beatrice quickly shook her head. "No point in you getting cold. It'll be fine. And I'll pick up some wood on my way back in. By then the fire will probably need some more."

With that, Beatrice pulled her coat, gloves, and hat back on and headed for the cabin.

The cabin definitely didn't feel as cozy as it had when it had heat. At least it kept out the wind—mostly. Beatrice realized that there were a lot more drafts inside than she'd realized when the heat was running. The drafts weren't as bad as the wind that was howling against the windows, but they weren't fun. She rolled some towels and put them on the window sill nearest the bed. Then she locked the door to the cabin. If Piper needed her, she was sure she'd knock, and would continue knocking if for some reason Beatrice was in a deep sleep. She pulled her bed further away from the window and then climbed under the covers, throwing the blankets she'd taken from the lodge on top of herself.

Beatrice fell almost immediately into a hard, deep sleep. When she woke up, she was a bit disoriented, not sure exactly where she was. Had there been a noise outside? She listened hard, wondering if the noise she'd thought she'd heard was what had finally roused her from sleeping. She didn't hear it again, although she strained to listen.

But she swore it had sounded like someone trying the doorknob.

Chapter Eighteen

Listening some more, she heard nothing. Maybe it had simply been the wind pushing against the creaky door to the cabin. It wasn't as if there weren't sounds all around her—the wind coursing through the trees, gusting against the small cabin. It was still pretty miserable weather.

Beatrice lay in the bed a few more minutes to see if she could fall back asleep again. She didn't seem to be able to, though. She pushed away her coat sleeve and glove to see what time it was. She raised her eyebrows. An entire hour had passed. She'd clearly really needed that sleep.

Beatrice got up and collected her blankets to take back with her to the lodge. Then she opened the cabin door and stared.

There were footprints outside. Footprints leading not only to the cabin, but footprints away, too.

Beatrice took a deep breath and tried to calm her pounding heart. The ice had changed back over to snow and was coming down pretty hard. She'd told herself that some of the footprints were just her own. She looked at the tread on her boots and then at the prints in the snow. Her prints were very faint and quickly becoming covered up by snow. No, these others were someone else's.

Maybe Piper's? But Piper would have knocked on the door, wouldn't she? Beatrice told herself that Piper might not have wanted to wake her up. Maybe she just looked through the window to make sure her mother was all right before moving back to the warmth of the lodge. One thing she knew—if it *had* been Piper, she'd say something to her when she went back inside.

And Beatrice *did* move quickly toward the lodge to get inside. She suddenly felt very exposed out here at the cabin, despite the needed sleep she'd been able to get.

She arrived back at the lodge a few minutes later. Everyone was quilting now, and it was very quiet inside the building. Lucy, the golden retriever, was happily lying on Georgia's feet near the fireplace. The quilters appeared to have compiled a stack of different fabrics and notions and looked as if they all could work on crazy quilts. The women glanced up when she came in, but no one mentioned having come over to the cabin. Piper, who looked tired herself, gave Beatrice a smile as she came in.

She noticed that Piper had indeed refreshed the wood on the fire, so she headed over to sit down instead of worrying about more wood. It looked as if it would last awhile. Piper gestured for her to sit down next to her, and Beatrice did.

"Everything okay?" asked Piper, giving her mother a searching look.

Beatrice must have still looked unsettled from what had happened at the cabin. She hesitated. If she told Piper the truth, she'd worry. Unfortunately, it was the kind of worry when you couldn't actually do anything to fix the problem unless Piper surgically attached herself to Beatrice.

"Everything is good," she finally said.

"Did you get some sleep?" asked Piper.

"I sure did." Beatrice paused. "Actually, I locked the cabin door, just to be on the safe side. I was thinking maybe I shouldn't have done that—you might have needed something inside."

Piper shook her head. "No, I've got everything I need right here. I didn't bring any extra fabric with me, so I didn't need to go to the cabin to collect it. The others made quick trips out to grab whatever extra fabric and tools they had. Glad you were able to rest for a bit. You deserve it."

Piper showed her the lively animal pattern on the project she was working on for Will. It was good that someone had brought a pattern that would work for children. She was hand basting the batting and the top layer so pins wouldn't get in the way of the hoop. Beatrice smiled and as she listened to Piper talking about Will, she felt herself start to relax. Maybe, she told herself, it was just someone from the group trying to check on her. Making sure she was all right. It might not have been anyone meaning to do her harm at all. After all, women were coming and going from the group regularly—headed to the dining hall for a snack or some water, or to get forgotten quilting supplies or books from their cabins. The person at her cabin door could have been completely innocuous.

Then her gaze moved over to the pile of boots. There was one pair that had snow melting off of them. Cora's red pair. All the other boots had puddles under them but no actual snow still attached.

Beatrice froze. Then she glanced at Cora. Could she have been the one who came to the cabin while Beatrice was sleeping?

Cora met her gaze and then looked away without concern.

Maybe Cora had just been checking on her, as she'd thought.

There wasn't much for the women to do except stay warm, quilt, and check on Starr. Time passed slowly, but all their quilting was making great strides. Beatrice spent the time thinking.

After a couple of hours had gone by, Beatrice stood up. "I'd better add more wood to the fire," she said to Piper.

Piper immediately stood up. "I'll do it."

"Let's do it together. I'd like to stretch my legs."

"Perfect," said Piper. "We'll get it done in record time. Maybe we can bring in an extra log or two to lay on the hearth so we don't have to brave the temperatures next time."

It was a short distance outside to the small shed where the wood was kept. However, the short distance meant for a frigid walk. The wind had no inclination to stop blowing as it moaned around them.

Beatrice slid open the door to the shed, and they stepped inside. They were removing the tarp from the wood pile when Piper suddenly stopped.

"What is it?" asked Beatrice with a frown.

"Do you hear that?" asked Piper quietly.

Beatrice did. It sounded like a very faint rendition of Twinkle, Twinkle, Little Star that was breaking up in parts.

"My phone," gasped Piper.

"Go inside! Maybe you can get better reception in there."

Piper darted off.

Beatrice grinned. If a phone call could make it through, perhaps everything else would start looking up, as well. Maybe the police and EMS could get to the retreat soon and take over investigating and providing help for Starr. She picked up a log.

She was about to set back after Piper when she found her path was blocked.

Chapter Nineteen

Cora stood in her way. At first, this just annoyed Beatrice. After all, she was holding a heavy log. "Excuse me," said Beatrice brusquely.

But Cora didn't move. Beatrice shifted the log and looked more carefully at the woman. She was very still, pale, and her expression was unreadable.

She couldn't know, could she? She couldn't realize that Beatrice suspected. She'd only glanced at her that one time after seeing the snow-covered boots.

"I need you to move," said Beatrice, keeping her voice from shaking with some effort.

Cora gave a short laugh. "Not going to happen. I can see you've figured it all out. Your friend was right—you apparently are a pretty good detective. Too bad you're not good at poker faces."

Cora was, though. There was no hint of her intent.

Beatrice opened her mouth to scream, but just then the whole lodge exploded with happy shrieks and screams. Apparently, they must have heard that help was on the way. Or perhaps the power had come back on with particularly bad timing.

So Beatrice did the only thing she could. She twisted around and drove the log straight into Cora's midsection. Cora left out an "oof" as her breath whooshed out. Beatrice dropped the log and ran.

She slipped and slid through the icy snow, desperation keeping her moving forward. Cora gave a furious grunt and headed silently toward her from the storage shed to the lodge.

Beatrice yelled out, “Help! Help!”

But the sound was still drowned out by the happy sounds inside. What was more, the wind was gusting so hard that it picked up her cries and carried them away.

Cora was a younger, stronger woman. She caught up with Beatrice. Then one of her feet shot out from under her and she fell, hard, on the icy surface of the ground.

Beatrice continued for the lodge, propelling herself inside.

The happy sounds stopped abruptly as the women all stared at Beatrice.

“Mama? What’s happened?” asked Piper in a fearful voice.

“Cora,” gasped Beatrice. “It’s Cora.”

Nicole stood. “Is something wrong with Cora? Is she hurt?”

“She’s the murderer,” said Beatrice. “She’s behind all this.”

Cora pushed through the door, gazing at Beatrice with loathing. She spat out, “Beatrice is the killer. She attacked me out there. I’d just gone out to help with the wood. She jammed a log into my stomach.”

Cora moved her clothing aside to show a huge red mark that was clearly going to bruise quite a bit.

“Did you do that?” asked Nicole, narrowing her eyes at Beatrice.

Beatrice tried to catch and control her breath. She was still winded from the run through the snow and all the screaming. “I did,” she said quietly. “Cora was going to kill me. Like she killed Aspen and Olive.”

Nicole put her hands on her hips. "It sure sounds to me like *you're* the dangerous one."

There were sounds of dissent from the Village Quilters. Savannah bellowed, "Not true!" Meadow stood up, unable to hear a word against Beatrice. "Beatrice didn't even know those women."

Nicole snorted. "Like Starr didn't know Aspen?"

Starr winced from her spot in front of the fire.

Cora said, "All I know is that I went out to help, and the next thing I know, Beatrice is attacking me for no reason."

Beatrice said in a quiet tone, "It was a sort of odd time to come help, wasn't it? Piper had just received a phone call. Help is, presumably, on the way. You told me you realized I knew you were behind the murders. That was your only chance to eliminate me before I could tell the police what I'd figured out."

Posy, her brow furrowed, said, "What did you find out, Beatrice?"

Beatrice said, "Well, for one thing, this wasn't the first time Cora tried to get me alone to get rid of me. When I was taking a nap this afternoon, someone tried coming in through the door."

"It was probably your daughter," scoffed Nicole.

Piper shook her head, her face ashen. "I was here in the lodge."

"At any rate, it's a good thing I locked my door. There were footprints leading away."

"But why?" asked Maggie. "Why on earth would Cora want to kill you?"

"That's what I want to know," said Cora with a huff. Her eyes were slits, and she looked at Beatrice with what might have been a warning.

"Well, there were clues scattered along the way," said Beatrice. "I'll admit that I didn't really put them together until I was in the lodge and saw that Cora's boots were the only ones that still had fresh snow on them. She was obviously the one who had come to the cabin."

Ivy said in a petulant voice, "Why didn't you say anything, then? You let us all hang out with a murderer this afternoon?"

Ivy was clearly already fine with having someone named as the killer. Even if it was one of her own guild members.

"I wanted to speak with some others first to decide how we were going to handle it if Cora was really the killer. At the time, if you remember, no one had been able to reach anyone from the outside. It's not as if we could safely confine Cora somewhere here. There isn't any heat."

"We still don't have any heat," said Ivy gloomily. "And no power, either. We just were able to hear from the cops that they're going to try to get here."

Piper said, "After Ash was able to get through to me and we realized there was a signal, Meadow reached the police dispatcher. They said help was on the way."

Beatrice nodded. "I wanted, privately, to come up with ideas for our next steps."

Nicole said, "Okay. So that's why you didn't tell anybody. What I want to hear is what made you decide Cora was the one who's been terrorizing the conference center. I haven't heard you say anything that would convince me she's behind all this."

Beatrice took a deep breath, still trying to recover from her sprint outside. "Well, let's look back at our first evening here. Aspen was bragging about her car, house, and lifestyle. Cora broke a glass."

"You call that a clue?" asked Nicole in disbelief. "Come on. I'd have probably thrown something at Aspen if I'd overheard her talking like that. It was typical Aspen. Besides, Cora can be clumsy. I've seen her drop things all the time."

"There were some pretty strong emotions playing across Cora's face. She looked furious," said Beatrice calmly. "And that made me wonder why."

Cora was staring implacably at her from across the room.

Maggie stepped in, impatiently. "Because she was jealous. We were all jealous of Aspen. Who wouldn't be? And furious, probably, because Aspen was being tacky enough to brag when we were all trying to make good impressions at a quilting retreat."

Beatrice shook her head. "But I think it was more than that. Cora has talked a little about her mother since we've been here. About her memory impairment and how she'd had to take her in. It's been very impactful on her."

Cora's face was still expressionless. A chill went up Beatrice's spine.

"Well, of course it has. It would for anybody. It doesn't mean that Cora killed Aspen because Aspen was rich and Cora wasn't," said Maggie.

Ivy glared at Maggie and Nicole. "I'd like to hear what Beatrice has to say. Don't you want this to be over? Because I do. If she's figured out who's behind all this, I'm going to be totally relieved."

Cora finally spoke up, spitting out venom toward Ivy. "That would suit you just fine, wouldn't it? Sending an innocent person off to jail. You're the one who had more motive than anybody."

Ivy gave her an icy look. "I certainly did not. Like I've said before, I wasn't happy about my husband's affair with Aspen. Clearly! But Aspen did me a favor in some ways because I figured out exactly what kind of man he was. It would have been even worse if I'd been the last one to know and everybody in town had been laughing at me. What a fool I'd have looked like. I had nothing to do with this. Nice try, Cora."

Miss Sissy growled at Ivy.

"What is with you?" Ivy hissed at Miss Sissy. "What's that sound supposed to mean?"

Beatrice remembered the argument Miss Sissy had mentioned. "She's remembering that you had an argument with Olive."

Ivy blew out a gusty sigh. "Over *firewood*. Olive wanted me to go on firewood duty. I reminded her that we are paying guests of the retreat and it wasn't my job to keep everybody warm here. Hardly something to murder someone over, despite what nutty old ladies think."

Miss Sissy growled again.

Beatrice said, "Ivy is right. Cora is trying to distract our attention."

Ivy sniffed.

"Going back to the glass Cora broke when Aspen was bragging about her lifestyle," said Beatrice. "Aspen made a comment at the time that Cora had trouble concealing her jealousy."

"As did most of us," said Nicole in that same, insistent tone.

"Later, I found out a little more about Cora. I found out more about everybody, of course, since we've all been stuck together. But one thing I found out about Cora was interesting. Her mother had lost her savings from internet scammers, due to her memory impairment. Cora's mom had to move in with her. I got the impression that Cora was very upset about this for a variety of reasons. She's having to do a lot of caregiving, for one, that she wouldn't have had to do if Cora's mother still had her savings."

Posy gave Cora a sympathetic look.

"Independence is important," said Cora in a level voice.

"Of course it is. And you're right to be upset. That's a horrible thing someone did to your mom," said Beatrice.

Cora snorted. "You have no idea. You can all pay lip service to feeling sorry, but you don't know what it's like to have your mother have her savings stolen from her. And these people don't care. They don't care at all who they hurt. It's like they're looking at their scams like a game—to see how much money they can get."

Nicole now sounded impatient. "Okay, I understand about Cora's mom. Yes, that's awful. But what does this have to do with Aspen or Olive?"

Meadow said huffily, "Beatrice is getting to that."

Beatrice said, "Aspen was one of those scammers, wasn't she?" She looked directly at Cora.

Cora pressed her lips together in a thin line.

"Wait. How do you know that?" asked Maggie. "Are you just guessing? Because it takes quite a big leap to draw that conclusion."

"After Aspen died, I went back to her cabin. The one she shared with Olive. I took a look at Aspen's computer," said Beatrice.

Nicole threw her hands up in the air. "Well, that's just great. When the cops finally do get here, you'll have contaminated the crime scene."

"That's not the place where Aspen was murdered. And I did use my gloves so as not to tamper with any evidence. I saw webpages that didn't make any sense to me at first. Later, Olive told me I was looking at the dark web."

"The dark what?" asked Meadow, looking confused.

"Web. It often acts as a sort of marketplace for illegal activity. Like purchasing credit card numbers or someone's identity."

Meadow's eyes opened wide. "Aspen was the one who stole from Cora's mom?"

"We don't know that. That's something the police could find out. She might not have. But whether she did or not, her activities made Cora furious. That's why she broke that glass. She was mad, and her fingers just reflexively tightened on the glass."

Everyone stared at Cora. Cora's mouth trembled a little.

Beatrice said in a gentler voice, "It might even have been an accident, right? Aspen had gotten up in the middle of the night and gone to the conference room. Maybe she was going to get started on a new quilt that would get everyone talking. Cora got up, too. I'm guessing that wasn't planned. Were you just wanting to go work on your quilt?"

Cora didn't speak, and Beatrice continued, "I couldn't sleep that first night, either. It's tough in a new place, isn't it?"

Cora stayed quiet, but Beatrice could see her wavering a little.

Beatrice coaxed, "So you went to the conference room, and you saw Aspen there. I'm guessing Aspen wasn't pleasant when she saw you since Aspen wasn't really pleasant to anyone. Did she needle you over something?"

Cora was silent still.

Beatrice said, "You were still bothered about Aspen's illegal activities. When she was bragging about all the stuff she owned and the trips she went on, all you could think of was your mother and how someone like Aspen had robbed from her. How did you find out about Aspen's scams?"

Cora said quietly, "I was at her house one day before the trip. I was collecting everyone's quilts for a service project the Sew and Sews were doing. Aspen walked into the back of her house to get the quilt, and I noticed that her laptop was open to something that looked really different. I walked over to take a quick look." She flushed and shrugged. "We were all sort of curious about Aspen. How she made so much money and could pay for the lifestyle she had. When I saw what was on her laptop, it looked fishy to me. I took a picture of the website with my phone. Later, I realized what she was doing." Her voice was bitter.

Everyone was silent in the lodge. You could hear a pin drop, despite the number of people in the room.

Beatrice continued softly, "It made you angry. Maybe you were waiting for a good time to approach her about it. When you walked into the conference room and saw her alone, it was the perfect opportunity." She paused. "I'm thinking you told Aspen you were going to tell the police about your suspicions. Maybe you were planning on showing the cops the photo you'd taken. Get them to investigate."

Cora nodded. Her voice was indignant. "*She* attacked *me*! Aspen was going to kill me. She changed in a split second."

"You didn't realize how dangerous she was," said Beatrice.

"No. She'd do anything to stop me from telling the police. She didn't want to go to jail."

"Tell us what happened next," said Beatrice.

Cora took a deep, shaky breath. "Aspen had a knife. I don't know why she had it on her. It was one of those wilderness-looking knives. Maybe she thought she'd be hiking, and it would be good to carry. Or maybe she was just the kind of person who walked around carrying a weapon. Anyway, she came at me with the knife. I was shocked. Totally knocked off-guard. All I could think about was trying to get away from her."

The women stared at Cora.

"I couldn't believe it," said Cora. "I thought Aspen would be defensive about her stealing. Because, it was *stealing*, just as much as if she'd gone to a bank and robbed it. She just stayed behind her computer and took people's identities and their credit card numbers. So I knew Aspen wasn't going to just roll over and tell me to just call the cops. But I figured she'd simply clam up and say I'd gotten everything wrong. Or maybe go and try to erase all her activity on her laptop. When she took that knife out, I didn't know what to think. I *couldn't* think."

Cora's hands were clasped and had tightened until they were white knuckled.

Nicole was staring at her in disbelief. "And then you killed Aspen."

Cora stared at her blankly, as if still living the moment with Aspen. "No. It wasn't like that. It was self-defense. She was attacking me, Nicole. Aspen was going to kill me with that knife and then erase all the clues leading to her."

"So what happened after Aspen pulled out that knife?" asked Meadow in a breathless tone.

Cora turned to her. "She lunged at me with it. I was still in total shock that Aspen planned on killing me. That was the last thing I thought she was going to do. I somehow got out of the way and deflected it with my arm. But Aspen was quicker than I was and much younger, too. She came right back at me again. It wasn't like I had any time to get away. I was pressed back against one of the long tables. I reached behind me to try to get my hands on anything I could use against her. The first thing my hand was able to grab were those shears." She paused. "You know the rest."

"It was self-defense," breathed Posy.

Miss Sissy barked, "Poppycock!"

Nicole looked wryly at the old woman. "I agree with you for the first time, Miss Sissy."

Cora said, "It *was* self-defense. It was killed or be killed."

"Sure," said Nicole. "But what about Olive? And what about the fact that you apparently were going to eliminate Beatrice outside just now? Would you call *those* times self-defense? Because I wouldn't."

Maggie said, "Tell us about Olive. I can't believe what you did to her. She was your *friend*."

Cora's expression once again had that blankness that made Beatrice shiver. "It was the same thing, Maggie. I had to defend myself."

Nicole looked skeptically at her. "So Olive threatened you with a knife? Because somehow, I just can't see Olive doing that, Cora."

Cora shook her head impatiently. "You don't get it. She wasn't threatening me with a knife. She was also threatening me with a loss of independence. With jail. What would happen to my mom if I were locked up and couldn't take care of her? She's the innocent party in all this. Mom doesn't deserve any of this."

Beatrice asked, "What did Olive know?"

Cora glared at Beatrice. "Well, apparently, she knew about the dark web stuff. You clearly came back to her and told her about it. She was able to put two and two together and realized Aspen was doing illegal stuff online. And, I guess, that I'd found out about it. Anyway, I knew I was going to have to keep Olive from saying anything to protect my mom."

"And Beatrice?" Meadow sounded very indignant now. "What were you going to do to Beatrice?"

Cora shrugged as if that was completely inconsequential. "It was the same problem. I needed for her not to tell the police what she'd found out. I knew if Olive had figured it out based on hearing about Aspen's activities, that Beatrice probably would, too. It was just hard to get Beatrice alone. You're all like pack animals."

Piper reached out and held her mother's hand, giving it a squeeze.

Beatrice said, "You tried to slip into my cabin while I was sleeping. The same thing was going to happen to me that happened to Olive. Except you didn't doctor my drink like you doctored Olive's. You were getting bolder."

Cora didn't say anything in response.

Nicole said slowly, "You said you locked the cabin door? So then Cora had to try to kill you when you were outside getting wood. But your daughter was there."

Piper squeezed Beatrice's hand again.

"Right," said Beatrice. "But Piper's phone rang inside. We could hear the ringtone from out at the shed. It was a sign that we could get a signal. She hurried off to get the phone. I guess Cora was watching and knew I'd be by myself with Piper inside the lodge." She shrugged. "I had to use self-defense, myself. I don't know how Cora was planning to kill me because I didn't give her the chance. I hit her with the log before I could find out."

The women all stared at Cora again. Her face was inscrutable in the light from the fire.

Cora finally said, "Okay. So here's the way it is. Aspen and Olive aren't coming back. They're gone. I'm really sorry about Olive. Aspen was something of a waste, as far as I'm concerned. There's no point in telling the police you've figured this out. It's not going to bring those women back. All it's going to do is to make things tough for my mom."

Nicole raised her eyebrows. "And for you. Because you'll be in prison."

Miss Sissy snarled.

"You can't tell the police," Cora explained calmly. "My mother doesn't deserve to lose me."

"I somehow didn't realize how totally narcissistic you are," said Ivy.

That was pretty remarkable, coming from Ivy. Beatrice's opinion of Ivy was that she was fairly narcissistic, herself.

"You're right, Ivy," said Nicole. "That's exactly what Cora is. Look at it this way, Cora. Olive didn't deserve to lose her life. I don't think Aspen did, either. Aspen was a pain, and she obviously broke the law and hurt a lot of people in the process. But she didn't deserve to die. She deserved to spend some time in jail. And you're not a judge and jury—you don't get to determine who lives and dies. That's for courts to decide. So of course we're going to tell the cops."

"You can't," said Cora, sounding ominous.

"You can't take all of us on," said Nicole with a short laugh. "Good luck. Even if you could, don't you think the police would find it a little obvious who the killer was if you were the only one left?"

Beatrice said, "What's more, the police would have to run their own investigation. They'd likely draw the same conclusion that Olive and I did. But it would be much worse if they decided that an innocent person had been involved in those deaths. There were others here with motives."

Cora was resolute. "Not going to happen. I can't have this happen to my mom."

Nicole threw up her hands. "Your mom is going to be fine. She has memory impairment. I'm sure the authorities can find a good memory care unit for her to go where she will have excellent care."

Cora was shaking her head. She suddenly made a dash for the door and struck out into the wintry weather.

Chapter Twenty

Nicole jumped up to go after her, but Maggie put a hand across hers. "Let her go, Nicole. There's no point in any of us getting hurt or freezing to death out there. The cops are on their way, right?"

Meadow said, "Apparently, they're able to get on the roads. At least they're trying to."

Nicole stood up and walked to the lodge door, locking it.

"What are you doing?" asked Starr. She'd been quietly sitting by the fire, looking pale and drawn during the scene. Now she sat up a little, staring at Nicole.

"Isn't it obvious? I'm locking the door."

Starr shook her head. "It's getting dark out there. We don't know that the police are on their way. Cora might try to retrace her steps and get back here to get warmed up."

"Well, too bad about that," said Nicole sarcastically. "She should have thought about that before she murdered two people."

Posy shifted nervously. "Maybe we should allow her to come inside. If we don't, we're just as bad as she is."

Nicole's expression changed as she considered this. "True. But I don't want her coming back in here and trying to kill one or more of us."

Beatrice said, "Let's take turns staying up this evening. Then, if she comes back, we let her in but maybe we figure out a way to confine her to a particular area of the lodge. The police are on their way, but they're clearly taking their time in order to make it here safely. Maybe we should try to get some rest. Aside from whoever is on the first shift, of course."

That was decided as the plan. Meadow offered to take the first shift. She busily worked on some hand-stitching by the light of the fire as the others pulled their bedding back out onto the floor and fell into light sleeps. Although it was dark outside, it was definitely not bedtime. But the stress caught up with the women and they tried to rest.

Beatrice didn't think she'd be able to sleep much at all, which had been the theme to her entire stay at the retreat. Plus, she'd had that nap during the afternoon. But she somehow managed to drift into a restless sleep. She was waking at the slightest sound, though. Considering she was in a room packed with other people, there were plenty of sounds to wake her.

Then there was a more ominous one. The sound of the door to the lodge opening up. No one in the group had gone out on a night like this . . . no one but Cora.

Sure enough, Meadow was saying, "Come on in. Don't be silly. You'll die out there."

And Cora, shivering and looking half-frozen, came slowly inside.

Beatrice stood up and walked over to Cora. Cora gave her a baleful look. Beatrice said quietly, "You'll understand if Meadow and I make sure you don't have any weapons on you."

Cora gave a short, bitter laugh. "You think I came to a quilting retreat with weapons?"

"I'm not sure. But you certainly could have taken one from the kitchen while you were here," said Beatrice.

Meadow nodded, her eyes wide.

They made sure Cora didn't have anything in her pockets, then let her sit by the fire. She held out her hands to the flames.

Piper had woken up by this time. It was amazing that no one else in the room was stirring. It must be exhaustion, due to the stress of the whole situation. There was definitely nothing comfortable about the setup in the lodge.

Piper joined them at the fire, looking at Cora cautiously. "Everything okay?" she asked.

"For everyone else maybe," said Cora in that same, bitter tone.

Beatrice ignored her. "Meadow, have you tried to call out again?"

That's because, after the initial elation of Piper's phone call and a bunch of successfully completed calls, they'd lost the cell phone connection again. The police didn't know that Cora had confessed in front of all of them.

Cora narrowed her eyes.

Meadow glared at her. "Don't you dare try anything." She said to Beatrice, "I tried once, but didn't get through. I'm trying not to use up my phone's charge now, just in case."

Beatrice said, "Mine still has plenty of power." She walked back to her sleeping pallet, picking her way gingerly among the sleeping quilters. Having retrieved her phone, she joined them again.

And the call made it through. A dispatcher on the other end told her that a car in the previous team had wrecked their vehicle but that another had set out some time ago.

Beatrice hung up, breathing a relieved sigh. She nodded to the others. "They're on their way."

No sooner had she said the words than they heard the sound of engines and saw headlights approaching the building.

The police had quickly and efficiently taken charge. Everyone woke up with a start before relaxing and cheering at the sight of the emergency workers coming in. Starr was immediately examined and put into a waiting ambulance. Cora was immediately put into custody, after her rights were read to her. A forensic team descended on the conference room and Olive's cabin. The police seemed confident that they'd find forensic evidence to back up the confession heard by the entire group.

The most exciting part of all was that they were all being transported back to the police station in a van to give statements and then be picked up by their families. They were told they could collect their vehicles later.

"What should we do about Lucy?" asked Beatrice. The golden retriever looked solemnly at her.

"You can throw her in the van, too," said one of the officers.

Posy quickly said, "I'll take her home with me until Starr is able to get back to the retreat."

They all quickly gathered up their things and headed out into the darkness without looking back.

The police station wasn't huge, and it was overwhelmed by the size of the group. But it had power, heat, and cell service.

Everyone was on their phones. Beatrice called Wyatt as soon as she'd gotten service. "Wyatt?"

"Beatrice! I've been so worried about you. Are you all right? Where are you?"

"It's a long story. I'm at a local police station. But yes, I'm fine. They're saying we can be picked up here. I've got to give a statement to the police first, but then I'll be ready to come home—only if it's safe for you to drive here." She gave him the address. "But don't come unless the roads are clear. I know it's dark and the lack of light won't help things."

Wyatt said, "The roads are better now, at least over in our area. I'll be there as soon as I can."

The station was full of chatter with the women calling their spouses and friends. Then a detective named Lieutenant Rogers asked Beatrice for a statement.

They were in a small room that was bare except for a table and a couple of chairs. He sat down with a laptop. "I've heard that you were the one who was trying to investigate what was happening."

Beatrice said wryly, "Well, I was doing my best. If it's any consolation, I tried very hard to make sure my efforts wouldn't derail anything you needed to do. I didn't mess with the crime scene or anything like that. I'm hoping you'll be able to get some good evidence that will stand up in court."

Rogers nodded. "I don't think that's going to pose a problem for us. Can you tell me what happened? And what you observed?"

So Beatrice walked him through the whole weekend. How Aspen had behaved and her impressions of her with the Sew and Sews. The fact that Cora had been very tense around her. How Beatrice had discovered Aspen's body and her illegal activities online. And what had followed with Olive.

Rogers was quietly typing the entire time, only pausing to ask questions. And to give her a bit of a hard time about Aspen's laptop.

"Sorry about that," said Beatrice ruefully. "I did try to be careful by wearing my gloves. I wouldn't ordinarily have interfered, but we weren't at all sure when the police would be over and we seemed to have a killer in our midst."

Rogers nodded. Obviously, he got it, even if he wasn't delighted about it.

She then explained the situation with Cora's mother. She paused. "It worries me a bit what will happen to Cora's mom."

"We've already been in touch with a social worker we often work with. She's fantastic and knows all the ins and outs of dealing with this type of issue. I'm sure she'll be able to help her mom with getting on Medicaid, looking at any life insurance policies to pay for long-term care, and that sort of thing. I have full confidence in her."

Beatrice nodded.

"Was there anything else you wanted to add to your statement?" Rogers asked.

But it seemed that, finally, Beatrice was done. And she wasn't only done with the retelling of the events of the weekend. She felt physically and mentally finished. That cloud of complete exhaustion rested on her again.

Rogers printed out the statement and got her to sign it. He collected all her information so that he could reach out and get back in touch again. Then she was free to go.

Minutes later, Wyatt arrived. His gaze jumped from one quilter to another until it rested on Beatrice. He rushed over and gave her a tight hug.

"I've been so worried about you," he murmured into her hair.

She hugged him even tighter. "I've been worried about you, too. And me," she said, laughing ruefully.

Piper came over to join them, having just finished giving her own statement. Miss Sissy, seeing her ride, came grumpily over, too.

Wyatt said, "Ash was getting ready to hop in the car with Will to come get you, but I told him to stay at home with the baby—that I could drive you over."

"Good idea," said Beatrice.

"Yes!" said Meadow, who'd overheard. "We don't want anything to happen to Will."

"Or to Ash," said Beatrice with a wry smile.

"Right," said Meadow, belatedly remembering her son.

"The roads are pretty good, but there's no point in making them get out in this weather," said Wyatt. "Meadow, I can take you back, too."

Meadow said, "Unfortunately, I need to wait on Ramsay. He said he wanted to have a word with the police here." She made a face. "Who knows when I'll be able to leave."

"What about you three?" Wyatt asked Posy, Savannah, and Georgia.

Posy said, "Oh thank you, Wyatt! But Cork is on his way. He should be here anytime now."

Piper, Wyatt, Miss Sissy, and Beatrice were about to go when Beatrice paused. "I should probably say goodbye really quick to the Sew and Sews. Especially since I had to suspect all of them of murder."

"We'll wait for you in the car," said Piper with a smile.

Miss Sissy growled, but didn't stop her.

Beatrice walked over to where Nicole, Maggie, and Ivy stood. "I'm heading out now. Have all of you got rides coming?"

The women nodded. Maggie said, "My husband is on his way to get Nicole and me."

Ivy made a small face. "And mine is coming to collect me. I'll have to give him the bad news that Aspen is gone."

Somehow, reflected Beatrice, Ivy didn't look all that sorry to be giving him the news.

"It's going to take a little longer for our rides to come than yours, of course," said Nicole. "Considering that we live farther away." She paused. "On a completely different note, I wanted to thank you for what you did."

Beatrice gave her a smile. "Thanks. I'm sorry about having to drag everybody through questioning like that."

Nicole smiled crookedly in response. "Yeah, it wasn't much fun being a murder suspect. But I get why you had to do it."

"And look at you," said Maggie. "You were able to figure it out."

Beatrice said, "Yes. But it doesn't make what happened any easier. I'm sorry about everything. I can't imagine losing two members of your guild."

Nicole gave a short laugh. "Actually, we lost three. Cora is gone, too. But we'll find a way to move forward. Do some recruitment for the guild or something."

Maggie said sadly, "I'm still having a tough time believing Cora did all this. Especially that she killed Olive. I mean, she and Olive got along really great."

"Yeah, but Cora was trying to protect her mom. Family comes first," said Nicole.

The sisters smiled at each other.

Ivy said petulantly, "Well, I for one am just glad she's locked up behind bars. We had a rough enough weekend without having Cora running around killing people. And now I've got to deal with things with my husband."

"What are you going to do? About your marriage, I mean?" asked Nicole.

Ivy blew out a sigh. "I'm going to divorce him. I clearly can't trust him. If he had an affair with Aspen, it could happen again with somebody else. There are other fish in the sea."

Maggie was quiet at this. Beatrice wondered if she were thinking about her own marriage and the husband that Maggie had cheated on.

Maggie finally spoke, echoing her thoughts. "You're right, Ivy. There are definitely other fish in the sea. I was thinking that on the drive here. There's more to life than money. And life's too short for me to be with the wrong guy. Plus, it's unfair to him that I'm not really all that committed to him. We can both find other people."

She didn't sound all that sure, though.

Beatrice said, "Well, it was good to meet you all. Sorry that it had to be under these circumstances."

Maggie made a shooing gesture at her. "You're good, Beatrice. Thanks for figuring everything out. Now go catch up with your hubby and daughter."

The women waved at her as she hurried out the door.

On the way out, Beatrice said to Posy, "Remember, I'll be there to give you a hand at the shop."

"Thanks! But give yourself time to relax first. We need to recover from our weekends," said Posy with a twinkle in her eyes. Lucy, the golden retriever, stood next to her and Beatrice reached down to give the sweet dog a farewell rub.

Wyatt was careful not to ask too many questions. He knew it had been a very stressful weekend and figured the story would come out in its own time. Instead, he answered all of their questions on the way back—how the weather had been (icy, but it had melted in their area) and, most importantly, how the baby was.

"I can't believe I missed his first snow," said Piper ruefully.

Beatrice chuckled. "I don't think he'll remember the milestone. You can take lots of pictures next time."

After finding out how everyone was doing at home, they fell into a companionable silence. Piper, perhaps in preparation of not getting much sleep at home, nodded off. Beatrice looked out the window into the darkness at the wintry landscape but the thankfully clear roads.

Once they'd safely dropped off Piper and watched Ash welcome her home with a huge hug (and a big hug from Will, too), they headed to Miss Sissy's house.

"S'mores," muttered the old woman.

Beatrice said, "I'm sorry the trip got so derailed. I know you were looking forward to having s'mores by the campfire."

Wyatt quickly said, "Why don't you come over tomorrow night? The weather is going to be clear, and I can fire up the grill. It might not be the same as cooking over a firepit, but I bet they'll taste just as good."

Miss Sissy grinned at Wyatt before practically skipping up her front walk and into her ramshackle house.

Finally, Wyatt drove them across the street to their cottage.

"Noo-noo and I have missed you," said Wyatt, his eyes warm as they looked at Beatrice. "We were worried about you."

"I was worried about me, too," said Beatrice with a smile.

She didn't know when she'd been so happy to be back home. The house was lit up with every light shining. Her corgi was beaming at her out the front picture window. And, when she got inside, Wyatt handed her a glass of wine and a plate of food he'd prepared before setting out to pick her up.

Later, sitting with Wyatt by a warm fire, wine in hand, she curled up beside him and felt the stress melt away.

About the Author

Elizabeth writes the Southern Quilting mysteries and Memphis Barbeque mysteries for Penguin Random House and the Myrtle Clover series for Midnight Ink and independently. She blogs at ElizabethSpannCraig.com/blog, named by Writer's Digest as one of the 101 Best Websites for Writers. Elizabeth makes her home in Matthews, North Carolina, with her husband. She's the mother of two.

Sign up for Elizabeth's free newsletter to stay updated on releases:

https://bit.ly/2xZUXqO

This and That

I love hearing from my readers. You can find me on Facebook as Elizabeth Spann Craig Author, on Twitter as elizabethscraig, on my website at elizabethspanncraig.com, and by email at elizabethspanncraig@gmail.com.

Thanks so much for reading my book...I appreciate it. If you enjoyed the story, would you please leave a short review on the site where you purchased it? Just a few words would be great. Not only do I feel encouraged reading them, but they also help other readers discover my books. Thank you!

Did you know my books are available in print and ebook formats? Most of the Myrtle Clover series is available in audio and some of the Southern Quilting mysteries are. Find the audiobooks here: https://elizabethspanncraig.com/audio/

Please follow me on BookBub for my reading recommendations and release notifications.

I'd also like to thank some folks who helped me put this book together. Thanks to my cover designer, Karri Klawiter, for her awesome covers. Thanks to my editor, Judy Beatty for her help. Thanks to beta readers Amanda Arrieta, Rebecca Wahr, Cassie Kelley, and Dan Harris for all of their helpful suggestions and careful reading. Thanks to my ARC readers for helping to spread the word. Thanks, as always, to my family and readers.

Other Works by Elizabeth

Myrtle Clover Series in Order (be sure to look for the Myrtle series in audio, ebook, and print):

Pretty is as Pretty Dies
Progressive Dinner Deadly
A Dyeing Shame
A Body in the Backyard
Death at a Drop-In
A Body at Book Club
Death Pays a Visit
A Body at Bunco
Murder on Opening Night
Cruising for Murder
Cooking is Murder
A Body in the Trunk
Cleaning is Murder
Edit to Death
Hushed Up
A Body in the Attic
Murder on the Ballot
Death of a Suitor
A Dash of Murder
Death at a Diner
A Myrtle Clover Christmas
Murder at a Yard Sale (2023)

Southern Quilting Mysteries in Order:

Quilt or Innocence

Knot What it Seams
Quilt Trip
Shear Trouble
Tying the Knot
Patch of Trouble
Fall to Pieces
Rest in Pieces
On Pins and Needles
Fit to be Tied
Embroidering the Truth
Knot a Clue
Quilt-Ridden
Needled to Death
A Notion to Murder
Crosspatch
Behind the Seams
Quilt Complex (2023)

The Village Library Mysteries in Order (Debuting 2019):

Checked Out
Overdue
Borrowed Time
Hush-Hush
Where There's a Will
Frictional Characters
Spine Tingling
A Novel Idea
End of Story

Memphis Barbeque Mysteries in Order (Written as Riley Adams):

Delicious and Suspicious

Finger Lickin' Dead

Hickory Smoked Homicide

Rubbed Out

And a standalone "cozy zombie" novel: Race to Refuge, written as Liz Craig

Made in the USA
Columbia, SC
19 March 2024